The Table of Regrets

The Table of Regrets: What Was Too Much?

FIRST EDITION

By Kimberly Cummings

Copyright

All rights reserved.

No part of this book may be reproduced in any form or by any electronic or mechanical means, including information storage and retrieval systems, without written permission from the publisher, except by reviewers who may quote brief passages in a review.

This is a work of fiction. All names, characters, places, organizations, and events are either products of the author's imagination or are used fictitiously. Any resemblance to actual persons, living or dead, or actual organizations or events is purely coincidental.

All Scripture quotations are taken from the King James Version (KJV) of the Bible.

Content Warning

This book contains depictions of violence, organized crime, addiction, and moments of emotional struggle. While these themes are handled with care, they may be difficult for some readers.

Note from the Author

The spiritual purpose of this story is to expose the consequences of pride, excess, and gluttony, and to point toward redemption, grace, and second chances through faith.

Dedication:

To God and my family.

"Whose end is destruction,

whose God is their belly,

and whose glory is in their shame,

who mind earthly things."

—Philippians 3:19 (KJV)

Contents

Chapter 1: Do We Have a Deal?

The basement smelled like old rain and rusted nails. Moisture beaded on the concrete walls and crawled in thin veins along hairline cracks, glistening under a single bare bulb that hummed and flickered like it was nervous to be here. A folding table sat crooked on one leg.

A drain in the center of the floor wore a black ring, as if the concrete itself had learned to hold its breath.

Asher Forest's wrists burned. The rope had been tied too tightly, and the coarse fibers bit deeper each time he shifted. His hands were pinned behind the chair, shoulders aching, fingers tingling with the numb-hot throb of poor circulation. Blood salted his lips. His left eye was a swollen slit that let light in the way a door on a bad hinge lets in wind unwillingly, irregularly, and with complaint.

"Do we have a deal?"

Grayson Rivers stepped out of the half-shadow as if he had been stitched from it. The men who'd done the beating flanked him, silent, patient, not even breathing hard. Grayson didn't need to raise his voice. He had the kind of calm that made other men want to be quiet, the kind of smile that meant he'd already decided what the ending would be and was only asking you to pick which road you preferred to get there.

On the streets of Central East City, people said his name with downcast eyes and short sentences. Ruthless. Untouchable. Efficient. The sort of man who wore a watch that cost more than a sedan and still checked the time like he was late for something important, like your life ending.

Asher blinked through the hum. The bulb's glow swam. He stared at nothing because nothing was safer than the eyes looking back at him.

"I said…." Grayson stepped closer and snapped his fingers in front of Asher's face. The sound cut the air in two. "Do you hear me?"

Asher flinched. For a second, his vision cleared, and the blue of Grayson's tie came into focus, deep, oceanic, maybe silk. He thought absurdly about how he could never afford a tie like that again. Not if tonight went the way the rumors promised.

"You need to sign over your business to me," Grayson said, almost conversational. "You've had your grace period. Time is up. You owe me money, Forest, and I always collect."

A drip from the ceiling plinked into the drain. The room's sound narrowed to that irregular metronome and Asher's own breath, which raked like sandpaper down his throat.

"No." The word came cracked. He swallowed against the iron taste. "I built it from nothing. From my aunt's basement. I wrote the first lines of code with a secondhand keyboard and a space heater that died every other day. That company is mine."

"Correction," Grayson said mildly. "It was yours. Debt makes beggars of kings, Asher." He patted his chest, as if searching for the right proverb among his ribs. "And beggars don't get to keep palaces."

The men behind him chuckled with two notes of ugly. One of them, the taller one with a healed split through his left eyebrow, dragged the toe of his boot across the concrete. It squealed.

Asher flexed his fingers, trying to feel them. He'd been trying to work the rope for the last ten minutes, rolling his wrists so the fibers might loosen. The skin there was raw, slick. If he could get his right wrist turned just so, he could maybe wedge it against the chair slat and….

"Look at me when I talk to you," Grayson said softly.

Asher forced his head up. He wished he could think around the throbbing. He wished his left eye would open all the way. He wished he hadn't taken the loan.

But grief is a backwards thing; it always arrives after the choice. He saw his aunt's kitchen in the eyes of his memory, its laminate counters worn to the pressboard at the corners, his laptop perched beside a cooling pie. She had moved around him like a planet, humming hymns from a Sunday morning long ago. Create in me a clean heart, O God, she would murmur, rhythm tapping on the table with a wooden spoon, and renew a right spirit within me. He wondered what she would say if she could see him now, if she would scold, or pray, or do both at once.

"I'm not signing," Asher said, and each word cost him.

Grayson's mouth tilted, and for a moment, there was something like admiration in his eyes. It lived there only long enough to prove it could. "Pride makes stubborn anchors," he said. "But anchors don't stop storms; they only drown ships."

The men behind him shifted again. The bulb flickered and steadied. A cockroach scuttled near the drain, froze, then darted into the safety of the grate.

"I'll make you a gentleman's offer," Grayson said, smoothing an invisible wrinkle from his cuff. "Sign the transfer papers. Walk away breathing. I take the company, and in return, you get to keep… breathing."

He made the word sound like a luxury item. Asher rolled his wrists, felt the rope seize a fraction, then give. He kept his shoulders slack, eyes heavy. "You can't run my software," he said. "You can own it, but it won't bend to you. It takes a different kind of loyalty to build what we built."

"We?" Grayson's eyebrows climbed. "If we're counting, your 'we' became my 'we' the moment you accepted my money." Your cash flow was drowning. You grabbed the first line tossed your way and forgot to ask who was holding the other end." He leaned in until Asher could smell his cologne, which was sharp, cedar cut with something sweeter. "Let's not pretend you didn't know who I was."

"I knew," Asher said, because there was no point in lying to a man who collected lies the way other men collected watches. "I knew, and I thought I could outpace you. I thought if I kept shipping updates, if I landed more city contracts…”

Grayson smiled for real then. “The city did love your demo,” he said. “Clean. Elegant. It would have been a shame for all that promise to… stall. Luckily, I have a way of getting meetings to go my way.”

Behind him, the shorter henchman lifted his chin and looked proud, as if he had personally nudged fate along with his knuckles.

Asher pulled lightly at the rope. The knot at the underside of the chair shifted. His right wrist found a sliver of space no wider than a coin. He stopped moving. He forced his breath into even counts, in and out, like he was back in that rented office scribbling deliverables on a whiteboard: scope, schedule, budget, risk. Risk. He almost laughed.

“What's it going to be, Asher Forest?” Grayson asked, stepping back, extending an empty palm like a man inviting someone to cross a street. “Pen or pine box?”

Asher's head rang like a bell. His left eye pulsed with heat. Somewhere beyond the walls, traffic whisper-hissed on wet pavement. He pressed his tongue to his busted lip and tasted copper. He felt the rope, felt the chair rail, felt the sweat slicking his skin.

He moved.

It was not graceful. It was not a plan. It was a reflex, a refusal dressed as instinct. His right wrist slid, skin peeling, tendons screaming. The rope caught, then slipped, then caught again, and he yanked his elbow like a man trying to break water after too long below. He surged off the chair. The wood groaned. The knot snapped. He didn't think. He was up and lunging, his shoulder a battering ram, his fist a hammer he had not earned but desperately needed.

His first punch landed with the soft-hard thunk of flesh meeting jaw. Grayson's head jerked to the side. Surprise flashed across his face, raw and human. For a heartbeat, the room forgot its script.

Then the room remembered.

The taller man hit Asher in the ribs. The shorter one clubbed him behind the ear. Asher stumbled, still half on his feet, swinging at air that would not cooperate. He saw Grayson's eyes refocus, cold pooling back into them. He saw the shape of a smile that didn't reach those eyes.

At all.

Grayson stepped forward and returned the favor. His knuckles drove pain deep enough to make the world white for a second. Asher folded back into the chair like a man thrown into himself.

"Enough," Grayson said, not loud, and the word rearranged the air.

He straightened his tie, touched the corner of his mouth with a thumb as if checking for blood, and found none. "I was hoping for civility," he said. "But hope is for churches and hospitals."

He waited until Asher's breathing slowed from panicked to merely wounded. He waited like a teacher waits for a classroom to quiet.

"I'm tired of the games," he said, voice flat now. "The company is mine. And you…" He lifted two fingers in a lazy salute. "You're done."

He did not look at his men when he made the statement. He didn't need to.

"Take him to Great Pond," he said. "Let him go for a swim."

The shorter one grinned. The taller one rolled his shoulders like a boxer warming up. They cut the rope from Asher's left wrist and yanked him up by both arms. Still dazed from Rivers' punch, his legs struggled to remember how to stand. The floor pitched like an ocean beneath him. The bulb flickered again, and when it steadied, Grayson had already turned away, checking his watch and moving on to his next appointment.

Asher found the table edge with his hip. They dragged him through a door that stuck, down a corridor lined with paint that had given up, past a stack of old tires and a rust-bitten shopping cart that looked like it was praying for death. Rain kissed his face somewhere between the last door and the night.

The alley outside was slick and narrow, its brick walls sweating with the day's leftovers. A streetlamp leaned crooked at the corner like a drunk shushing himself. The men shoved Asher toward a black SUV idling at the curb.

The engine purred with the confidence of a beast that had eaten before and expected to eat again.

He tried to plant his feet. A boot found the back of his knee. His leg collapsed, and they folded him into the back seat as if he were laundry they were late to put away. The door thunked shut. The world shrank to upholstery that smelled expensive and faintly of gasoline.

He stared at the headrest and thought about code, simple, beautiful things arranged in the correct order until the machine learned to behave. Then he thought about messier algorithms: choices, debts, the human heart miscalculating interest.

God, he thought, and the word surprised him by arriving. If you're listening, if you've ever heard…. help me. It wasn't eloquent. It didn't need to be.

The SUV slid through Central East City with the patience of a shark. Buildings turned their backs to the road… row houses lit from within, laundromats blinking tired neon, a bakery chalkboard promising fresh cinnamon rolls in the morning, if anyone made it that far. The driver kept the radio off. The wipers marked time with the rain. His knuckles popped one by one against the wheel. In the passenger seat, the shorter one scrolled through his phone, grinning at a joke only he would ever read.

Asher counted lights. He measured the distance to any door that might open. He saw himself, eight years younger, sitting cross-legged on the floor of his aunt's basement, his laptop warm on his thighs, a plate of leftover chicken wings sweating on a napkin nearby. He had written a note in permanent marker on the wall behind the cheap brown desk: Don't quit. Don't sell your soul. The note had felt brave then. Now it felt like a dare from a man who didn't know how dark the night could get.

The car turned off the main road onto a smaller one where the trees hung low and thick, their leaves whispering in the rain. The SUV's headlights caught the sign with white letters peeling off a green face: GREAT POND: 2 MILES. The shorter man smiled again, like a boy heading for a bonfire.

"Company field trip," he said.

The taller one didn't answer. His eyes found Asher in the rearview, steady and cruel, the way a man weighs a bug he may or may not crush.

Asher flexed his fingers. He was trying to feel them again. He rolled his left wrist. The rope was there, but his right hand had been retied, but tighter, smarter. He pressed his thumb against a fray at the knot. The fibers pricked like tiny teeth.

He breathed in. He breathed out. He tried the knot again. It did not budge.

The road narrowed until puddles became mirrors. The car turned down a rutted lane where grass dragged wet fingers along the doors. Branches brushed the roof. The engine changed pitch, laboring. Then the trees fell back, and Great Pond opened like a dark eye staring up at a darker sky.

Cattails lined part of the shore like a congregation waiting to sing. A floating dock drifted in its chain. The rain made rings across the surface, silver coins dropped into a black well. Somewhere far across, a frog croaked a single, skeptical note.

The driver turned off the headlights. The night took a long, slow breath.

"Out," the taller man said, matter-of-factly.

They hauled Asher into the rain. His shoes sank a little in the soft bank. The air smelled like wet earth and the kind of cold that seeps into the bones. He turned his head toward the tree line, toward the idea of somewhere else, anywhere else. A hand grabbed his jaw and wrenched it back.

"You tried," the shorter one said with a grin. "Points for effort."

He thought he could perhaps twist, perhaps run, possibly stumble toward the dock and then, what? Swim? With what strength? With what lungs?

Grayson wasn't here to watch this part. He never was. Delegation was a skill that had made him rich. Asher should have learned it better for himself, how to delegate trust to God instead of men with ledgers and long knives. He thought of a verse his aunt had stuck to the fridge with a crooked magnet: For what shall it profit a man, if he shall gain the whole world, and lose his own soul?

"This is unnecessary," Asher said, and the words came out soft, an apology to no one and everyone. "You'll get your money."

"Boss said swim," the taller man replied. "You don't argue with tide charts."

They marched him to the edge, where the bank gave way to water that kept its secrets. The rain hardened, as if the sky itself refused to listen. The taller man drew another rope and wound it around Asher's midsection in a quick, practiced rhythm, the knot tightening with a heavy clink.

Asher looked down. A half-cinder block dangled from the rope like a cruel punctuation mark. His body pitched forward, stomach knotting. He swallowed hard. The world tilted. The pond seemed to breathe.

"Hold still," the shorter one said, almost friendly. "We'll make this quick."

A laughable kindness bloomed in Asher's chest, small, bright, stubborn. He might have smiled if his mouth wasn't broken. "Quick," he said, barely a word. "I appreciate the efficiency."

The taller one frowned, uncertain if he'd just been mocked. The shorter one chuckled, delighted. "I like him," he told his partner. "Shame it won't matter. Let's end this before the rain comes down harder.

Asher stood in silence, his mind slipping back to his office, where a mug was stamped "KEEP SHIPPING" in block letters, and a corkboard displayed his aunt beaming, clutching their first LLC certificate as if it were a blue ribbon. He remembered the lines of code that had sung when he compiled them, the hum of the app beneath his fingertips, obedient and alive.

"Any last words?" the taller one asked, mock solemn.

Asher looked at the water. Rain fell steadily, relentlessly, like a faucet left on too long. The crickets were muffled beneath the patter on the dock. He lifted his eyes to the clouds, to where stars might have been on a brave night. Raindrops struck his bruises, each sting burning his raw skin.

"Yes," he said to them, or to God, or to the part of himself that hadn't yet gone quiet. "Forgive me."

"Aw," the shorter one said. "Church boy after all."

The taller man reached into his coat and drew something glinting…a knife, but not for show. For a second, Asher thought mercy had dropped into the scene like a coin from a stranger's pocket. Then cold metal slid into his side.

They shoved him.

The cold was instant, a baptism without a choir. The shock gnawed at his bones. The rope splashed heavily, tugging with a patient, merciless pull. Asher kicked. The brick argued for gravity, and his legs had no answer. Above him, the world blurred into a smeared oval of light and dark. He held his breath because breath was all he had.

His body remembered swimming from a summer when the world had been simple laughter on a dock, a dare, the slippery feel of algae on a ladder rung. He clawed at the knot. His fingers, clumsy and numbed, scraped hemp. He yanked, twisted, and felt the rope rasp skin from his waist. Dots of light burst in his vision, bright insects that seemed to come from inside his skull.

Not like this, he thought. Please, not like this.

Something brushed his ankle. A weed. A fish. An old
fear. He kicked again and felt the rope snag, however briefly,
on a root, a rock, some stubborn, blessed thing. The pull
changed. The brick swung. He used the swing. He leaned his
weight into the snag, grabbing at the rope with both hands,
trying to wedge it into the underwater cradle of whatever
had taken pity on him. The knot shifted. Pain spiked across
his ribs. The tug loosened just an inch, then two. He slugged
upward, lungs burning, head screaming.

His face broke the surface for a ragged instant. Air
ripped through him like fire on dry grass. He coughed up
water, maybe blood, sucked more in, and choked again. Rain
pelted his cheeks like thrown gravel. The shore was a black
seam, cattails just hinted in the dark. Ahead, the men
receded toward an SUV already forgetting him. They didn't
look back. Men with finished tasks seldom do.

He sank again, the brick arguing the facts.

He found the root with his knees this time, or it
found him. He jammed the rope into the crook of it and
pulled until the fibers screamed a song he had been waiting
to hear. One strand popped with a sound more felt than
heard. Another loosened, then slipped. He wriggled. He
pushed. He tore skin and did not negotiate with the pain.
The rope loosened enough for the brick to fall away, circling
down like a black moon.

His body rose, too tired now to call it swimming. He
drifted toward the reeds where the water kissed the mud.
Hands…his own, unbelieving…found the edge. He pulled

himself onto the bank like something newly born and not entirely grateful about it.

In the cattails, Asher lay on his side, chest heaving, blood leaking from his wound, rain freckling his face. The night was a bowl tipped to pour him out.

He heard the SUV idling in the distance, satisfied. He waited for footsteps returning, for the laugh, for the *just kidding*.

He stayed quiet, hidden in the cattails. He didn't dare lift his body; he couldn't risk them coming back to make sure he stayed under.

Then the vehicle faded into view on the main road. None came.

For a minute or an hour, he didn't move. Time was optional. Breath was not.

He rolled to his back, pressing on his wound and staring at the colorless sky. His left eye would not open at all now. His right blinked slowly. A moth worried the air above him, zigzagging toward a light that wasn't there.

"God," he whispered, the word a thread. "If You… if You have any mercy left for me…" He couldn't finish it. Maybe he didn't have to. The prayer had its own legs. Somewhere deeper along the bank, a twig snapped.

He tensed, or whatever version of tensing a broken body could manage. The cattails shushed each other in a wind he couldn't feel. Somewhere nearby, a dog barked once…. curious, then again…urgent. Blood mixed with rain on his tongue, copper and salt in every gasp.

He held still, listening. For a moment, his mind betrayed him: maybe they had turned the SUV around, come back to make sure he was gone for good.

A light? No… just the rain catching on a darker shape as it moved where the pond lipped the shore. He closed his eyes and let the sound pass through him. If it were them, it would be fast.

It wasn't them.

He didn't know how he knew. Maybe it was the hesitation, the small gasp, the whispered 'oh,' the way a human voice makes room in the night air…an air that slowly thinned into morning without his noticing.

Asher's vision tunneled, the world closing to a narrow corridor with a single door at the end. He felt himself sliding toward it slowly, inevitably. The last thing he registered before crossing through was a hand on his shoulder, warm, shaking; the grip of someone who wasn't there to hurt him.

Then everything went out like a light that had been waiting for permission.

Chapter 2: The Edge of Stillness

The sun had just begun to rise over the Great Pond, its golden light stretching across the rippling water. Birds were stirring, and the world seemed to move at a calm, unbothered pace until a frantic bark shattered the morning stillness.

A man walking his German shepherd froze when he noticed something unusual at the edge of the bank. His dog tugged at the leash, pulling toward what looked like a figure slumped on the damp grass. The man's stomach tightened as he drew closer.

"Oh, my goodness!" he whispered, though he didn't know him. The pale face, streaked with blood, looked lifeless. The man dropped to his knees, fumbling for his phone as his heart pounded.

"9-1-1, I need an ambulance at Great Pond, now! There's an unconscious young man. Please hurry!"

He kept his trembling hand on Asher's shoulder, trying to steady his own breathing while keeping the dog calm. Minutes felt like hours before the distant wail of sirens cut through the silence.

Paramedics rushed in, voices clipped and urgent. One checked Asher's pulse, another examined the swelling on his head.

"Unresponsive. Severe head trauma. Let's move now!"

The bystander stepped back, clutching his dog's leash, as they lifted Asher onto the stretcher. He felt helpless, yet he couldn't shake the image of that bruised face. He whispered a prayer under his breath as the ambulance doors slammed shut and the siren wailed into the distance.

At the hospital, fluorescent lights flickered above as doctors worked swiftly. Tubes, wires, and monitors surrounded Asher's still body. The beeping machines filled the room with an eerie rhythm, the only sign of life in him.

Hours passed, but Asher did not wake. A nurse, scanning his medical records, found a name under the emergency contact list: Keith Forest, father.

She picked up the phone, steadying her voice before dialing. "Mr. Forest? This is St. Central East General Hospital. Your son Asher has been admitted. His condition is very serious. I recommend that you come to the emergency department as soon as possible."

The weight of those words hung heavy in the air. Somewhere across town, Keith Forest's world shattered in an instant. Keith stood frozen in his kitchen, the receiver pressed against his ear long after the nurse's voice had faded. His mind struggled to process the words: very serious…admitted… come as soon as possible.

His chest tightened, and the weight of fear settled in his gut. He had always prepared himself for calls about late bills, work troubles, even neighborhood gossip, but never this. Never his son.

His hands trembled as he reached for his phone again, scrolling through the familiar list of numbers. His finger stopped at one name: Carolina Becker, his daughter.

He pressed the call button. Three rings.

"Dad? It's early, what's wrong?" Her voice was warm but quickly sharpened with concern when she heard his shallow breathing.

"Carolina…" His voice cracked. He gripped the counter with his free hand. "It's Asher. He's in the hospital. They said… his condition is very serious."

Silence filled the line, broken only by Carolina's gasp.

"Oh, Lord, have mercy. Which hospital? I'm coming right now."

"St. Central East General," Keith managed, his throat dry. "They said I need to get there fast."

"I'll meet you there," she said firmly. "Dad, listen to me, you drive safely. Don't lose yourself on the way."

Keith closed his eyes, trying to steady his shaking hands. "I don't know what I'm about to walk into, Carolina."

"Then you won't walk into it alone," she answered.

He nodded even though she couldn't see him. Hanging up, Keith grabbed his keys, the world around him blurring. For the first time in years, he whispered a prayer under his breath, the kind he hadn't spoken since he was a boy.

And then he walked out the door. The drive to St. Central East General unraveled in fragments of traffic lights, the sweep of headlights, the hollow sound of his own breath. Keith gripped the steering wheel until his knuckles blanched, cars streaking past like comets. His daughter's voice echoed in his mind: Don't lose yourself on the way. But his heart was already breaking apart.

He swung into the emergency room lot, killed the engine, and rushed inside. The sliding glass doors parted, releasing a wave of antiseptic sharp enough to trigger memories. A nurse met him halfway, already recognizing his face from the records. "Mr. Forest? Your son was brought in unconscious. He's receiving care right now. The doctor will speak with you in just a moment."

She guided him to a row of stiff plastic chairs along the wall. The clock above the reception desk ticked too loudly, every second stretching like an accusation. He clasped his hands together, knuckles whitening, staring at the floor tiles as if they might hold an answer. He waited.

Minutes later, footsteps approached. A woman in a white coat stopped in front of him, her expression composed but heavy. She extended her hand.

"Mr. Forest? I'm Dr. Levin, one of the attending physicians in the emergency department."

He stood quickly, nearly knocking the chair back. "How's my son?"

She took a careful breath, choosing her words. "Your son suffered severe head trauma. We were able to stabilize him, and his breathing and heart rate are steady, but he's not regained consciousness." Her voice softened. "Right now, he's in a coma."

The word landed like a blow. His chest tightened as though the waiting room had lost all its air.

Dr. Levin continued gently, "We'll be running further tests and monitoring him closely. The next twenty-four hours are critical. I know this is overwhelming, but we'll keep you updated every step of the way. Would you like me to take you to see him?"

Keith swallowed hard, his throat too tight to form words. He followed the doctor down the corridor, past flashing monitors and muffled conversations. Inside the room, she gestured to each part of Asher's body as if pointing out a human body model. "There's swelling in the brain. We're monitoring closely. Right now, he's not responding to external stimuli. But we'll do everything we can."

Asher lay in the hospital bed, pale and motionless, tubes and wires clinging to him like vines. His face was bruised, his lips split, his body unnervingly still. Machines beeped in a steady rhythm, a cruel reminder that it was the hospital's equipment, not his strength, keeping him alive. Keith's chest collapsed in on itself.

"What happened?" he whispered, stepping closer, his voice breaking. "Who did this to you?"

He reached out, trembling, and laid his hand on Asher's. The skin was cool, limp, and unresponsive. Keith's knees weakened, and he sank into the bedside chair, gripping his son's hand with both of his own.

Suddenly, the beeping, the sterile smell, and the low hum of machines all dragged him backward in time.

Fifteen years earlier, he had sat in a nearly identical chair, holding the hand of his wife, Amelia. Her eyes had dimmed from the cancer that ravaged her body, her voice reduced to whispers. He remembered the way her hand grew colder each day, until the day it went still forever. He remembered the helplessness, the rage, the hollow silence that followed.

And now here he was again. Another hospital room. Another loved one slipping away.

Keith bent forward, pressing Asher's hand against his forehead, his shoulders shaking. "Not again," he muttered hoarsely. "I can't lose you, too."

His tears dripped onto Asher's skin, vanishing into the stillness of his son's body.

The chair creaked beneath him as he collapsed fully into it, grief clawing its way out of his chest. The weight of the past and the terror of the present pressed down until all he could do was grip Asher's hand tighter, as if by holding on, he could keep him from slipping further away.

And for the first time in fifteen years, Keith Forest let himself break.

Chapter 3: The Call That Couldn't Wait

Carolina Becker sat at the edge of her bed, the hospital's call still ringing in her ears. Her hands shook as she scrolled through her contacts and pressed on the name she always turned to when life fell apart: Robin Meyer, her mother's twin sister.

When Robin answered, her voice was full of warmth, carrying the lilt of Ireland through the line.

"Carolina! What a surprise. How are you, love?"

Carolina's throat tightened. "Aunt Robin… It's Asher. He's in the hospital. He's…He's in serious condition."

There was a sharp intake of breath. "Oh, dear God. Tell me where you are."

"I'm home, now. Getting ready to leave."

Carolina's eyes stung.

Robin went quiet, her breath shaky on the other end. "I'd come this second if I could. But you listen to me, Carolina, stay close to your father. Don't let him carry this alone. And stay by your brother's side. He'll need you more than ever."

Carolina nodded, wiping her eyes though her aunt couldn't see. "I just wish you were here. You've always known what to do when everything fell apart."

"You'll know too," Robin whispered firmly. "Because you're stronger than you think. Now go. Be with him."

Carolina hung up, clutching the phone to her chest. For a brief moment, she felt fifteen years old again, the day their mother died, the day Aunt Robin stepped in as the anchor of their shattered family. And now, once again, the storm was raging.

She grabbed her coat and keys. It was time to face the hospital. Robin hung up the phone with her niece, her hands trembling. She turned toward her husband, Daniel, who was sipping coffee by the window of their rented cottage in Ireland.

"Daniel… It's Asher," she whispered, tears streaming down her cheeks. "He's in the hospital. Serious condition."

Daniel set his cup down immediately. "What? How? Did she say what happened?"

Robin shook her head. "No details. Just… It's bad." She pressed her hands together, trying to keep them from shaking. "We have to go home. I can't sit here while Carolina and Keith face this alone."

Daniel rubbed his forehead, pacing the small room. "Flights are packed. we might not find anything for days. But we'll try. We'll cut the trip short if we can."

Robin sank into the chair, her entire body trembling. "Fifteen years ago, when Amelia died, I swore I'd never let those kids go through something like that without me. And now look…" Her voice broke. "Carolina's thirty now, Asher twenty-eight, but they're still my babies."

Daniel crouched beside her, his own eyes glassy. "We'll do everything we can. Somehow."

The two of them sat there in silence, puzzled, terrified, already scrolling through flight schedules, desperate for answers that wouldn't come fast enough. Meanwhile, on the other side of the Atlantic, Carolina pulled on her coat and drove through the early morning sunlight toward the hospital. The roads blurred through her tears, her heart hammering against her ribs. When she finally arrived at the hospital, the front desk clerk asked her name and quickly called a nurse.

"Carolina?" the nurse confirmed gently. "Come with me. He's just down the hall."

Carolina nodded, unable to trust her voice. She followed in silence, the echo of their footsteps carrying down the sterile corridor. At the end, the nurse pushed open a door to a dimly lit room.

The sight of her younger brother shattered her.

"Asher…" she gasped, covering her mouth. Tears welled immediately, spilling down her cheeks. His bruised face, the wires, the machines, it was more than she could bear.

Keith stood from the chair, his own eyes swollen. He gently touched her shoulder.

"I…. Carolina, I didn't want you to see him like this."

She stepped forward anyway, brushing her hand across Asher's arm. "What happened?" she whispered. "Dad… he's too young for this. We're too young for this."

Keith nodded, his jaw tight. "I know. Believe me, I know."

Together they stood, side by side, as the machines beeped steadily in the background, father and sibling bound by grief, both wondering how much more loss their family could endure. The hospital room was unbearably still. The steady beep-beep-beep of the heart monitor was the only sound. At last, Keith lowered himself into the chair, his hand gripping Asher's, while Carolina remained standing at the foot of the bed, frozen. Neither spoke. Words seemed useless, too fragile for the reality in front of them.

Carolina wiped her face with the back of her hand, her breath catching as she stared at her brother. His chest rose and fell in a shallow rhythm, machines doing most of the work. Bruises shadowed his jaw and temple. She wanted to say something, but her throat closed every time she tried.

The silence pressed in, thick and suffocating, wrapping around the three of them…. father, daughter, and the son caught between life and death.

Then, the door creaked open.

A nurse stepped inside, carrying a small tray of supplies. Her shoes squeaked lightly against the polished floor as she approached the bed.

"Excuse me," she said softly, her tone gentle but professional. "I just need to check his vitals."

Keith straightened, releasing Asher's hand reluctantly, as though letting go even for a second might allow him to slip further away. Carolina backed up, her arms crossed tightly against her chest.

The nurse worked quietly, adjusting the IV, jotting down numbers on the chart, and shining a small light into Asher's eyes. "No change," she murmured, almost to herself.

Keith's voice cracked through the silence. "When… when will we know if he wakes up?"

The nurse hesitated, her expression careful. "It's hard to say. Head injuries vary. Some patients wake up in hours. For others, it takes days… even weeks. But right now, he's stable. That's the best sign we can hope for."

Carolina swallowed hard, her eyes fixed on her brother's still face. Stable didn't feel like comfort; it felt like limbo.

The nurse gave them both a sympathetic glance before slipping quietly out of the room, leaving the silence to settle once again.

Keith leaned back in the chair, his hand finding Asher's once more. Carolina finally moved closer, sitting on the opposite side of the bed. Their eyes met briefly, heavy with fear neither of them dared to voice. The room had settled again into silence after the nurse left. The steady rhythm of the machines seemed louder now, filling every corner with a reminder of Asher's fragile state. Minutes passed. Neither moved. Neither spoke. The silence pressed down until Carolina could no longer bear it.

Her voice cracked as it broke the air.

"I feel like it's Mom lying there," she whispered, her lip trembling. "Not Asher."

Keith's head turned slowly toward her. His brows knit, but he said nothing. Carolina kept going, her words spilling before she could stop them.

"When Mom died, I was fifteen. I thought I understood loss, but I didn't. I never told you this, Dad… but the day she passed, I felt like my whole chest caved in. Like someone had stolen air from me and I'd never breathe again." She brushed at her tears with the sleeve of her coat. "I hated the hospital. I hated the smell, the sound of machines, even the way the floors squeaked. I hated everything, because it all meant she wasn't coming back."

She inhaled sharply, steadying her voice. "The only thing that got me through was Aunt Robin. She stepped in when we were broken, and it made the pain just a little less sharp. I knew she wasn't Mom, but I knew that every time I looked at her and seeing her face, hearing her voice… it felt whole, even if it wasn't complete. The way she loved us, it was more than enough."

Keith swallowed; his throat was thick. His voice was gravelly when he finally spoke. "She did step up. More than

36

I ever asked. More than I could have done alone. She gave you both what I couldn't when I was too buried in my own grief."

Carolina nodded, staring at Asher. "She gave us hope. And he… he clung to her basement like it was his world."

Keith's eyes softened at the memory, and before he could stop it, the past came flooding back.

***

He saw Asher at thirteen, huddled over an old computer Robin had salvaged from a neighbor. The basement smelled faintly of paint and laundry detergent, the dim light buzzing overhead.

Keith remembered leaning on the doorframe, watching his son with equal parts confusion and awe. Asher's small fingers tapped furiously at the keyboard, his brow furrowed in deep concentration.

"What are you doing down here all the time?" Keith had asked, trying to keep his tone casual.

Asher didn't even glance up. "I'm building something."

"Building what?"

"A game. Or maybe software. I don't know yet." His voice was quick, clipped, and full of excitement. "I learned some coding online. Look, if I type this, the whole screen changes." He turned the monitor so his dad could see rows of strange letters and numbers filling it.

Keith had no idea what any of it meant, but when Asher finally looked up, his eyes glowed with fire. That look of raw, unstoppable passion was unmistakable.

Keith had walked back upstairs that night, shaking his head but smiling. He didn't understand it, but he knew his son had found something bigger than himself.

The flashback faded as Keith blinked, staring at the pale figure before him now. The boy who once filled a basement with light and energy lay still, silent, his future suspended in uncertainty.

The room fell quiet again, the weight of memory pressing into the present. Father and daughter sat across from each other, bound by grief, tethered to hope, and haunted by the silence that refused to break.

Chapter 4: The First Drift

The silence of the hospital room stretched into Asher's mind. Somewhere beneath the hum of machines, his subconscious stirred, tugging him away from the present and into the shadows of his past.

At first, it was music. Heavy bass thumped in his chest, neon lights streaked across his vision and sweat dripped from bodies pressed too close. He remembered the laughter, the liquor burning his throat, the rush of lust and adrenaline. He was untouchable or at least, he believed he was.

Night after night blurred together: stumbling out of clubs with friends, collapsing onto couches he didn't recognize, kissing strangers whose names he never bothered to ask. The emptiness afterward was always louder than the music had been. But he drowned it again and again, bottle after bottle.

And then, one memory sharpened against the haze, his college graduation.

He could see it clearly. His father's backyard was full of family, with balloons tied to the fence and food spread across long tables. Keith had shaken his hand with tears in his eyes, Aunt Robin's smile wide with pride. Even Carolina, who rarely fussed over him, had hugged him tighter than usual.

That night, he wore the glow of accomplishment. He had made it, a degree in software development. His father and aunt believed in him, trusted that he had his future in his hands.

But when the party ended, and the house grew quiet, Asher's other life came calling.

He told his father goodnight and promised Aunt Robin he'd get some rest before tomorrow. Then he slipped away into the city, five of his college buddies waiting in a car already echoing with laughter.

The local bar was packed, overflowing with graduates who felt invincible. They drank, shouted, and sang over each other. Asher downed shots until the room tilted, until his chest was buzzing with that familiar, reckless thrill.

When they piled into the car, none of them should have been driving. But the line between fun and danger had blurred long ago. Tires screeched, voices slurred, the world outside flashing by in streaks of light.

Then red and blue sirens. The sharp wail of police brakes cutting through their drunken haze.

Asher remembered the officer's voice, stern and clipped. "Step out of the vehicle. You've had too much."

Hours later, he sat in the holding cell of the police station, head pounding, throat dry. His friends had already called their families. He stared at the payphone, dread crawling through him. He couldn't call Dad. He couldn't call Aunt Robin.

His hand shook as he dialed Carolina's number.

By the time she reached the station, her pulse was racing as fast as her thoughts. The sound of his broken voice over the phone hadn't left her. She arrived with her hair pulled back hastily, her expression frozen in a state of shock. She had never seen him like this. She had never even known he drank.

"Asher… what have you done?" she whispered, her eyes red as she signed the papers for his bail.

He had begged her there in the dim hallway of the station, his voice cracking with desperation..

"Please, don't tell Dad. Don't tell Aunt Robin. I swear this was a mistake. I won't drink again…. I promise."

Carolina hadn't answered him then. She had only stared, her disappointment cutting deeper than anger ever could.

Asher's chest burned as the memory replayed, the shame heavy in his gut. Because the truth was, he had broken that promise. Again, and again.

The sound of the holding cell door echoed in his subconscious until it dissolved into nothing. His mind fell silent once more, dragging him back into the stillness of the coma. The room had gone quiet again, thick with the kind of silence that makes your ears ring. Keith kept his hand on Asher's thumb, moving without rhythm over the back of his son's knuckles. Carolina sat opposite him, elbows on her knees, eyes fixed on the rise and fall of Asher's chest like she could steady it.

A soft rap at the door.

Keith flinched. Carolina straightened.

The door opened just enough for a broad shoulder and a badge to appear. A man in a charcoal jacket stepped in, shutting the door behind him with deliberate care.

"Mr. Forest? Ms. Becker?" he said, voice even. "I'm Detective Kramer. I'm sorry to intrude. I won't take much of your time."

Keith stood as if pulled by a wire. "Is there…" He swallowed. "Is there news?"

"Nothing I can share yet," Kramer said, calm, practiced. "Right now, I'm confirming background, routine questions. It helps us move faster." He glanced at Asher, then back to Keith. "I know this is difficult."

Keith nodded stiffly. "Ask what you need."

Kramer opened a small notebook. "Your son's full name is Asher Michael Forest, twenty-eight. Lives alone? Or with someone?"

"Alone," Keith said. "Townhouse on Larkspur. He keeps it clean. He's…" Keith's jaw trembled; he forced it still. "He's a good kid. He built his own software company from the ground up. He doesn't drink, doesn't touch anything he shouldn't. Works late. Keeps to himself. Never had trouble with the law."

Kramer's pen paused. He lifted his eyes. "Never?"

Keith's spine stiffened. "Never."

A beat of air hung between them.

Kramer turned a page in the notebook. "Mr. Forest, I want to be respectful. But I need the most accurate picture I can get." His voice didn't sharpen; it softened, which somehow made it worse. Records indicate your son has been arrested three times for driving under the influence. The first was six years ago. The most recent was last year."

Keith blinked. The words didn't land all at once; they struck in fragments that didn't make sense until they did. He gripped the arm of the chair so hard it scraped against the floor.

"What?" His voice cracked into the room. "Three… DUIs?" He shook his head. "No. No, that's…Asher doesn't drink."

Across the bed, Carolina closed her eyes like she'd been waiting for this moment to punch through the wall. When she opened them, they were wet.

"He told me he would stop," she said quietly.

Keith turned to her, confusion curdling into something raw. "Carolina, what are you talking about?"

She swallowed. "The first time. He called me. After graduation." Her gaze slid to Asher, then to the floor. "I bailed him out. He begged me not to tell you. He promised it was over."

Keith's face drained. "You knew?"

"Only the first one." The words rushed out, too fast, as if speed could soften them. "I thought it was a mistake. I believed him."

"Why did you keep something like this from me?" Keith's voice rose, rough and hoarse. "I'm his father."

"I was trying to protect my brother." She wiped at her cheek with the heel of her hand. "You were still grieving, Dad. I didn't want to break you again."

"How is that helping him?" The question cracked in the air. Keith's hand shook as he pointed…at Asher, at the tubes, at all of it. "Keeping secrets isn't protecting him. It's enabling him. And now look at him."

Carolina flinched as if the words carried weight. "So, this is my fault now?" she whispered. "Is that what you're saying? That he's here because of me?"

"Enough," Kramer said gently, stepping closer to the foot of the bed without crowding them. "I'm sorry you're hearing this from me. I'm not here to place blame or cause problems. I'm here to document what's true so we can find out who did this to your son."

The room breathed twice, and neither father nor daughter realized they were holding.

Keith's shoulders sagged. He pressed his palm to his eyes, then dragged it down his face. "I understand," he said, voice smaller. He looked at Kramer. "Please… continue."

Kramer nodded. "I'll keep this narrow. Has your son mentioned recent conflicts? Arguments? Changes in his routine? Anyone new…. personal or professional, who seemed to be circling him?"

Keith shook his head numbly. "He worked. He visited on Sundays when he could. He brought his laptop everywhere. That's who he was." Carolina hesitated, her voice low. "It seems like he only got better at hiding things." She shook her head, guilt pressing at her chest. "After that first DUI, he never let us see a stumble, and then he picked up two more without us knowing. Now… I can't help wondering what else he kept from us. Who he really is when we're not looking." Kramer jotted a quick note. "Understood." He jotted down Keith Forest and Carolina Becker's numbers, then closed the notebook not with finality, but with care. "I'll leave my card. If anything occurs to either of you…texts, names, places…. call me anytime."

He set the card on the tiny rolling tray beside the chart, then looked at Asher for a long, even second. "We're working this," he said, and it landed without bravado, just a fact.

Keith nodded once. "Thank you."

Kramer reached for the door, paused. "I'll check in again later today." He gave them both a slight, respectful nod and slipped out, the door kissing shut behind him.

Silence swept back in, heavier than before.

Keith stared at the card as if the numbers on it might rearrange into answers. Across the bed, Carolina wrapped her arms around herself, fighting the cold that had nothing to do with air conditioning.

After a time, Keith lowered into the chair and found Asher's hand again. He didn't look at his daughter when he spoke.

"I should've known," he said, voice frayed. "I should've seen him. All that time, and I didn't see him."

Carolina's reply was barely a breath. "Me either."

They stayed like that three breaths, two voices, one steady monitor while the questions Detective Kramar hadn't asked, and the truths he hadn't told, crowded the small room and pressed against the glass. Keith sat rigid by the bed, the detective's card resting untouched on the tray. His chest rose and fell in short, uneven bursts. Carolina sat shifting in her chair, her fingers knotting and unknotting in her lap before she drew her arms tight around herself. Her eyes stayed fixed on the floor. The silence pressed between them like a wall.

Minutes blurred into hours. The hallway beyond the door filled and emptied again with the rhythms of hospital life—shoes squeaking, carts rolling, a muffled voice calling for a doctor. Shadows lengthened on the floor tiles, stretching across the room as afternoon bent toward evening. Finally, she spoke. Her voice was small, breaking.

"Dad… I'm sorry. I should have told you about the first DUI. I thought I was protecting him. I didn't want to pile more hurt on you after everything we'd already lost."

Keith's head bowed, his shoulders sagging with the weight of her words. He rubbed his hand over his face, the anger softening into exhaustion.

"I know. I just…" His voice cracked. "I feel like I failed him, Carolina. I didn't see it. I didn't see any of it. And now…" His eyes flicked to Asher's still body. "Now I'm sitting here wondering if I'll lose him too."

Carolina's throat tightened. She pushed up from her chair and crossed to his side. "We both missed it. Maybe because we wanted to believe he was okay. Maybe because we were scared of the truth." Her hand brushed his arm. "I'm sorry for keeping that from you. I didn't mean to hurt you."

Keith turned to her slowly. His eyes, red-rimmed and tired, searched hers. After a long moment, he nodded. "And I'm sorry for snapping at you. My anger isn't at you. It's on me. At all of this."

They sat in silence, both looking at Asher, the machines filling the space between their breaths.

"Emotions are high," Carolina whispered. "We're scared. That's all this is."

Keith placed a hand on her shoulder and gave it a gentle squeeze. "You're right." He glanced toward the door. "I need some air. Just for a minute."

Carolina nodded. "Go. I'll stay with him."

Keith lingered a second longer, then leaned down and pressed his palm once more against his son's hand. His jaw tightened, his eyes closing as if in prayer, though no words came. Then, with a weary sigh, he straightened and walked out into the hallway.

The door clicked shut softly behind him. Keith lingered a moment in the corridor, drawing a long breath as if the air outside the room might be lighter. When he turned, Detective Kramar was there, his notebook tucked under one arm, his expression steady but not unkind.

"I wanted to circle back, as I said I would," Kramar began, lowering his voice out of respect for the quiet around them. Keith nodded, his jaw still set, but his eyes flickered with a trace of weary gratitude. "I don't have anything new yet," Kramar admitted, his voice low. "But I want you to know we're moving. We've pulled footage from street cameras near the park entrances, and we're working with the city to check any cameras by the lots and the boathouse at Great Pond. We're widening the net, anyone who came or went, we'll know."

Kramar went on, "This isn't being pushed aside, Mr. Forest. We're treating it as an active and urgent matter. I'll keep you informed, even if all I have to report is that the work is ongoing." He slipped another card into Keith's hand, pressing it there firmly. "You think of something, anything…you call me. Day or night."

Keith studied the card, then looked back at the detective. His voice was low, rough. "Thank you. It helps to hear that."

Kramar gave a short nod, almost like a vow. "You focus on your son. We'll focus on the rest."

The detective moved off down the hall, his steps measured, leaving Keith standing in the hush of the hospital's fluorescent-lit corridor.

Back in Asher's room, Carolina was sitting beside her brother. The silence returned, heavier now, wrapping itself around the room like a shroud.

Chapter 5: All We Have

Carolina sat alone in the room, her father's footsteps fading down the hallway until only the steady hum of machines remained. The silence pressed against her, louder than any argument, heavier than the truth Detective Kramer had left behind.

She leaned closer to the bed, her eyes locked on her brother's still face. "You promised me," she whispered, her voice sharp with hurt. "Do you remember that night, Asher? You looked me in the eye and swore you'd stop. And I believed you."

Her fingers gripped the edge of the blanket, knuckles whitening. "I defended you. I carried that secret, even when I hated myself for it. And you kept drinking anyway." Her voice broke, a sob catching in her throat. "Do you know what that did to me? I trusted you… and now I find out you were still drinking, still tearing yourself apart?" The tears came fast now, streaming unchecked down her cheeks. She pressed a hand to his arm, her body shaking with the weight of it. "You can't die, Asher. Do you hear me? You can't. We are all we have left. Me. Dad. Aunt Robin. We need you. I need you. Please… please wake up."

Her words hung in the air, unanswered. The monitor beeped on, indifferent.

The silence grew until it folded in on itself, and Asher's mind opened again.

The bass hit first, pounding through his chest. Laughter, slurred voices, the clink of bottles. He was back in a crowded bar, lights flashing, bodies pressed shoulder to shoulder. He felt the burn of alcohol slide down his throat, familiar and warm, and the haze of recklessness that followed.

He stumbled out into the night with friends, their arms slung over each other's shoulders, voices raised in drunken song. Tires screeched, headlights blurred, and then red and blue sirens.

Another DUI.

He sat in another holding cell, the taste of metal and regret sharp in his mouth. But this time, he didn't call Carolina. He didn't call anyone. He told himself he'd figure it out, that it wasn't worth the shame of letting her down again.

Weeks later, it happened again. Another night, another blur, another arrest. His stomach churned as he signed the release papers, guilt crawling through his veins.

For a moment, Carolina's face flashed in his mind the look she'd given him that first night, the weight of her disappointment. You promised me.

But he shook it off.

"She won't find out," he told himself, numbing the voice with another drink.

The laughter, the neon lights, the burning liquor swallowed the guilt whole.

And then, silence again. The silence swallowed the room, and, inside it, Asher's mind tipped again past the holding cells and the fluorescent nights into motion and miles.

Airports. He remembered the soft roar of jet engines and the way a boarding pass warmed in his palm. Conference badges. Hotel lobbies that all smelled faintly the same. He told himself he was networking. Landing deals. "Just drinks with a client," he'd say, or "One celebration with the team." But the lines blurred: a handshake over a demo in the afternoon became a shot glass clacked against another at midnight.

Riverfront City: a rooftop lounge, windswept and loud, his blazer catching the breeze while he laughed too hard at someone's joke. Desert City: the club, a cavern of bass, his phone buzzing with messages he hardly read, bodies moving like the dark had no edges. Harbor Town: a narrow bar with sticky floors and a jukebox older than he was, his shoulders loose, but his judgment looser.

He started telling himself the same story over and over…I earned this. I'm young. This won't touch the work. The story worked until mornings arrived with dry mouth and a skull that felt split along invisible seams. He missed a breakfast meeting once and lied about food poisoning. He pushed a demo to late afternoon and forced a smile through the throb. The investors still nodded. The orders still came in. Success covered sins like paint over water damage, for a while.

One night in Harbor Town, a shoulder clipped his as
he squeezed toward the door, a spill sloshing across the toe
of someone's boot.

"Watch it," a man snapped.

"I said my bad," Asher muttered, past patience, past
careful.

"You're gonna buy me a drink for that."

"Already bought too many," Asher shot back, and
the space between them narrowed. There were two of them;
one leaned forward, breath sour with whiskey.

"What'd you say?"

Asher smiled that loose, reckless smile he'd been
practicing for years. "I said, find a towel."

A fist flashed hard and quick. His mouth flooded
with copper. Someone shoved him against the wall, and his
shoulder popped with a hot line of pain. He swung back on
instinct and hit nothing but air. Glass shattered. Voices rose;
a bartender yelled. The bouncer was moving. Asher ducked
sideways on wobbly legs and found the thin metal bar of a
service door with his palm.

He burst into the alley, breath ragged, night air
snapping cold against his sweat. He ran… past dumpsters,
past a humming transformer, past a cat that bolted into the
shadows. He didn't stop until the alley forked to a loading
dock behind a warehouse. A sliding door sat grooved in
steel, the platform vast and silent. He scrambled up, heart
banging, and tucked himself behind a stack of empty pallets.

Somewhere behind him, the service door slammed open, and two voices spilled into the night.

"Where'd he go?"

"Forget it. Let it go."

Their footsteps faded. Asher stayed where he was, back pressed to wood, lip bleeding, chest heaving until the dark thinned and his shoulder hung out of place. He told himself he'd rest for a minute and then find the car, drive to the hospital, let someone pop it back in. But the night folded over him like a tarp. When he woke, it was to the rattling whine of a rolling door and the clatter of boots. A slice of early light cut across the concrete. Three men stood at the edge of the dock in reflective vests, blinking at him like he was a stray dog someone had forgotten to shoo.

Asher looked up with gummy eyes. "Where am I?" he croaked, his voice gravelly.

All three men still staring at him, surprised and a little amused.

"Man, you must've been hammered," the first said, setting down a toolbox.

"Yeah, if you don't know where you are?" the second added, eyebrows climbing.

The third squinted. "What are you doing here? You need to call somebody to pick you up."

Asher rubbed his eyes, trying to scrub the grit from his brain, searching for a street sign that wasn't there. The warehouse smelled of cardboard and stale coffee. His lip throbbed when he touched it, and the memory of the bar flared fists, glass, the door, the run.

"Uh… I'm not from here," he muttered. "I'm from Central East City."

"Wow, man, you're about three hours from there," the first said, whistling low.

They laughed, not cruelly, just incredulously.

"Yeah, he was wasted," the second said, shaking his head. "How'd you even get here?"

"Oh…I came with some friends," Asher said, the lie assembling itself, rickety and familiar.

The third snorted. "Some friends you've got. They bailed on you." Asher braced a palm on the dock and pushed himself up. The world tilted, his knees hollow. He pitched forward; two of them caught his elbows and steadied him.

"Easy," the second one said. "Sit a second before you face-plant."

"Ouch, my shoulder," Asher muttered, staying on his feet. He gripped it, remembering it was still out of place.

The first one frowned. "My bad… what happened to you last night, seriously? "Uh… I was kinda in a bar fight," Asher said, voice uneven. "Two guys chased me, and I ducked in here, hid between the pallets. My shoulder popped in the fight, and my lip got busted." He touched the swelling as if to prove it.

The third man let out a low whistle. "Man, you had a rough night. I can pop that shoulder back in for you." Asher hesitated, then let him do it. The guy guided him to lean back against the wall and hold still. With a sharp jolt, the shoulder slid back into place. Asher rolled it carefully, almost like it hadn't been out at all. "Thanks."

"No problem," the man said. "Been there before. Saved you a trip to the ER."

"We should get him inside," the first one suggested. "Let him make a call. Get some coffee in him." "I don't want to get in trouble," the second said, his glance fixed on the open door, where the faint spill of light reached across the dock. "Let's just leave him out here."

"We can at least bring him some coffee," the first countered. He jabbed a finger toward the dock. "Wait here…we'll grab you a cup." They disappeared into the warehouse. Asher eased himself back onto the boards, staring at the grooves etched into the wood by years of freight. He pressed his fingers to his split lip, eyes watering. The fight flickered through his head in jerky frames. He could still feel the jolt of his shoulder, the sting in his mouth, the way the alley had swallowed sound behind him.

This has to be it, he told himself, chest tight with the thought. No more drinking. I mean it this time. I'm done… *I have to be.* The promise felt clean for the span of a breath. It always did in the morning.

The men returned with a paper cup and a phone charging brick, mercy in small, practical pieces.

"Here," the first one said. "Careful. It's hot."

"Thanks," Asher murmured, the heat grounding his shaking hands. "You got a ride?" the first one asked.

"No, but I'll call a car service." He pulled out his phone. Dead. Asher dug the charging cable from his suit jacket. The first man brought over a charging brick and handed it to him, letting him plug into the dock's port. The black screen lingered for a moment before the battery icon finally flickered to life.

"Thanks," Asher muttered, embarrassed he'd shown up with half the solution.

In the glass, his reflection stared back: swollen lip, bruised cheek, a stranger in a suit jacket that had seen the floor of too many bars. When the phone had enough life to connect, he dialed a car service. While he waited, one of the men leaned against a pallet, studying him.

"You a salesman or something?" the man asked.

"Something like that," Asher said. Easier than explaining code and contracts, easier than unpacking how his name meant different things to different people. After twenty-five minutes, the car finally pulled up, idling at the curb. Asher stood, steadier now, and lifted the cup in a small salute. "Thanks for the coffee," he said.

"Get home safe," the first man told him. "And maybe don't come back to this dock."

They grinned. He tried to grin back. It hurt.

In the back seat, the city slid past, washed out and, honestly, the kind of morning light that showed everything the night had tried to blur. Asher peeled his jacket sleeve back and stared at the faint smear of someone else's drink dried near the cuff. The vow tightened in him again like a belt. No more. Enough.

He made it through that day on coffee and sugar, and two showers. He pushed the demo back and apologized convincingly. He sent Carolina a text: "Busy week." Call you Sunday. He didn't mention the lip or popped shoulder. He angled his face on the video call with a client, so the shadow hid the bruise. He put in ten hours and told himself he'd outrun it with work.

The next city didn't care about his promises. Neither did the people in it. Travelers kept moving, and nights had short memories. An old classmate recognized him at a hotel bar weeks later—congratulations, shots, a crowd he didn't know by midnight and wouldn't remember by morning. He laughed too loudly and said yes too easily. He danced with strangers and tipped too much. I earned this, he told himself, a flimsy umbrella held over a storm.

He kept his distance from anything that felt like consequence. He hired a car instead of driving. He walked when the street was bright enough. He told himself he was being smart now. The second DUI lived like a warning label at the edge of his mind; the third sat beside it like fine print. When guilt surfaced—as it did, uninvited… Carolina's face came with it, the way it had looked under the harsh lights of that first station hallway.

You promised me.

She won't find out, he argued with the same stubbornness that let him grind code for sixteen hours straight. He tucked the thought away like he tucked receipts he never read into a pocket he never emptied.

The invitations kept coming. Industry parties. After-hours. Softly lit lounges where deals were whispered and gossip moved faster than music. People mistook stamina for character all the time.

Sometimes, he avoided the bar entirely yet still found trouble. A house gathering after a conference turned hazy; a balcony that felt too close to open air; someone he didn't know offering something in a palm, and his easy, early no. He hadn't crossed every line. He kept telling himself that it mattered.

There were quieter nights, too, hotel room curtains drawn against the city, a bottle alone. Those were the ones that should've scared him most and didn't. The noise had become a habit; the silence had, too.

When he finally went home for a weekend, he left the lip healed and the bruises fading on a life he didn't bring through the door. Aunt Robin asked if he was eating enough. Dad asked about the latest release, the contracts. Carolina asked if he was sleeping. He said yes to all three and passed the roast. They talked about schedules, football, and a neighbor who'd decided to plant tomatoes too late in the season. He let the warmth of it drape over him and pretended it could last without work.

Then the calendar filled again. He ran fast because the track was smooth and well-lit and because the speed kept him from looking down.

When the following invitation arrived, a message with an address and a winking promise, he held the phone too long before typing: 'Sure.' The vow at the loading dock weakened in the glare of the screen. He told himself he'd leave early. He told himself he'd alternate water. He said many things to himself.

He made it to midnight. He made it past. The dance between guilt and numbness picked up where they'd left it, partners who never needed introductions. In a bathroom mirror he didn't recognize, he touched his mouth where the scar had become a thin, rough line. He smiled at himself and didn't like the way the smile looked. He turned away and went back out to the music anyway.

Back in the hospital room, Carolina brushed her thumb over a spot on Asher's forearm where a faint mark lived that she'd never noticed. The monitor ticked time without comment. Her voice had gone hoarse with pleading; now it was gone altogether. She sat with him and let her tears dry into tight salt along her lashes.

In Asher's drifting mind, the noise finally thinned. The scenes slowed, then stilled. The vow at the loading dock echoed once, twice, then faded into the same wide quiet that had swallowed everything else.

Silence retook the room, steady, indifferent, complete.

Chapter 6: Through a Father's Eyes

The hours crept by inside the hospital room. Carolina hadn't moved much since her father left for air, only shifting in her chair when her legs cramped or when she brushed her fingers against the stiff blanket covering Asher's body. The tears that had poured from her earlier had dried into tight salt at the corners of her eyes, leaving her face raw, her throat sore.

The monitors kept on in their steady rhythm, beeps and hums indifferent to the ache in her chest. Afternoon light pushed through the blinds, cutting sharp lines across the wall, bright enough to remind her that the world outside was still moving. People were shopping, walking dogs, sitting down for lunch while her world had been reduced to a single bed, a limp hand, and the cold truth that nothing was promised.

Carolina leaned forward, resting her elbow on her knee, her chin in her palm. She stared at her brother's face, bruised and silent, and tried to remember the last time she'd really looked at him. Not at his photos online or in the business magazines that occasionally ran his story but really looked. The shape of his mouth, the small scar near his hairline from when he fell off his bike at eight, the faint shadows under his eyes that she had ignored at the last family dinner.

She had spent so long believing he was invincible. Now all she could see was how fragile he really was.

The door creaked open behind her.

Carolina glanced up quickly, expecting maybe the nurse again, but it was her father. Keith stepped inside slowly, shoulders heavier than before, his hands shoved deep into his pockets. His tie was loosened, and his jacket was draped over his arm. His eyes, once sharp and fiery, looked older in the sterile light. He stood for a moment near the door before quietly pulling it closed behind him.

Carolina sat up straighter. She had braced herself for anger, his words from earlier still stung, but his face was softer now, almost fragile.

He came closer, stopping at the foot of the bed. For a long while, neither of them said anything. He just looked at his son, the rise and fall of his chest, the wires, and the bruises. His throat worked like he wanted to speak but couldn't.

Finally, Keith exhaled. "I've been walking the halls. Thinking. Remembering."

Carolina nodded faintly, waiting.

Keith moved around the bed and lowered himself into the chair he had occupied earlier, rubbing his forehead with the heel of his palm. "When Detective Kramer walked out of here, I felt like the floor gave out under me. I've always believed Asher was different. Better. That he didn't let the world touch him the way it tried to touch me. Or you." He shook his head. "Hearing about those arrests… I didn't want to believe it."

Carolina swallowed, her chest tight.

"But" Keith continued, "after I cooled off, I realized maybe I was clinging too tightly to the picture I wanted to see. Not the whole picture." He looked up at her, eyes tired. "I was too hard on you. I shouldn't have snapped the way I did. None of this is your fault."

Carolina blinked against a fresh sting of tears. She nodded quickly, unable to find words.

Keith leaned back in the chair, eyes drifting to the ceiling tiles. "Still… none of it changes what I feel about him. Or you. You both lost your mother far too young. And still, you both grew into something remarkable."

Carolina's lips pressed tight, her eyes on her brother.

Keith gestured faintly toward Asher. "Look at what he's done and built a software company from scratch. Signed deals with people I couldn't even dream of meeting. Brought in millions before he was thirty. People discuss him in boardrooms and in articles. I used to sit at the kitchen table, reading his name in print, and I'd think…. that's my boy. My son did that." His voice faltered. "He doesn't deserve to be lying here."

Carolina looked at him sharply. "Dad…"

"I know, I know." Keith raised a hand, shaking his head. "None of us deserves what life throws at us. But after losing your mother, fighting through the grief, he didn't let it kill him. He turned it into a drive. And look where it carried him." He gave a weak smile. "The polished version, at least."

Carolina sat back, her arms folded tightly. She wanted to scream that it wasn't the whole story, that his success was stitched with cracks her father couldn't see. But she stayed quiet, pressing her lips together until the thought dissolved.

Keith's gaze softened as it drifted to her. "And you. Don't think that I don't see you. After your mom died, you stepped up. You helped me keep the house together, you helped your brother with his homework, and you even made sure I ate when I forgot." His eyes grew wet. "I didn't thank you enough for that. But you were just as strong as he was. Maybe stronger."

Carolina blinked fast, tears rising again. "I didn't feel strong, Dad. I felt like I was holding everything with shaking hands. I still do."

Keith reached across the bed and set his hand over hers. "Shaking hands still holds."

The words hung there, steadying something fragile between them. Keith leaned back, his voice distant, as if slipping into memory. "I can't shake the picture of Asher first starting with computers. Aunt Robin gave him that old desktop from her neighbor and set it down in her basement. That boy spent hours on it. I'd peek down the stairs over and over, to watch him hunched there, typing like the thing would vanish if he blinked."

Carolina smiled faintly. "I remember the glow from the screen under the door."

Keith chuckled low. "One night, I asked him what he was doing. He looked up, face all lit up, and said, 'Building something.' I didn't understand a word on that screen, just lines of numbers and letters. But I understood that look in his eyes. He was on fire. I knew right then he'd go further than I ever could."

Carolina looked at her brother, her chest tightening. She could almost see that boy in the pale face lying before her.

Keith sighed, rubbing his temples. "He worked his way out of grief by throwing himself into that computer. While other kids played ball or chased girls, he was down in that basement, writing code. Your aunt used to bring him sandwiches and leave them on the step. Half the time they'd be cold before he remembered to eat them."

Carolina laughed softly through her tears. "That sounds right."

Keith's face softened. "When he launched his company, I thought… finally. We made it. After everything life had taken from us, we had something to show for the fight. He didn't give in. He built a life." His voice thickened. "That's why this feels so wrong. He doesn't belong in this bed. Not him. Not after all that."

The room went quiet again, but the silence was gentler this time, not as suffocating as before.

Carolina leaned forward, her hand still on Asher's blanket. "Dad," she said softly, "we're proud of him. But maybe he was carrying more than we knew. Maybe we all are."

Keith looked at her, a shadow of something unspoken in his eyes. He nodded slowly, not pressing further.

The clock on the wall ticked past one, early afternoon settling heavy in the room. Keith pushed himself up from the chair with a groan, slipping his jacket back over his arm.

"I need some coffee," he said quietly. "Maybe some air again." He looked at her, his expression tender. "I'm proud of you both. No matter what happens here. Don't forget that."

Carolina's throat closed around her reply, but she managed to make a nod.

Keith gave her shoulder a gentle squeeze, then leaned over his son one more time, pressing his palm against the back of Asher's hand. His lips moved like he wanted to say something, but no sound came. After a long pause, he straightened and walked toward the door.

The soft click of it shutting left Carolina alone once more.

She sat still, staring at her brother, her chest aching. "Dad doesn't know everything, Asher," she whispered, her voice barely audible. "But I do. And I don't know what to believe anymore."

The monitors beeped on, steady and indifferent. Outside, the afternoon sun shifted its angle, drawing longer shadows across the floor.

The silence returned, deeper than before, and the day wore on.

Chapter 7: The Taste of More

The steady beeping of the monitor was the only sound in the hospital room. Carolina sat with her chin in her hand, watching the faint rise and fall of her brother's chest. Keith had stepped out for air again, his absence leaving the room hollow. The silence stretched, deep and restless, until Asher's mind opened once more.

It was greed's first bite when he was twenty-five when he signed his first major deal. The ink dried on the contract, and suddenly, his small software company was no longer just a hopeful startup; it was a player. Orders stacked up, clients lined up, and the money flowed faster than he had imagined.

At first, Asher told himself he was just ambitious. He wanted security, stability, something his family never had after his mother died. But ambition quickly soured into something sharper, hungrier.

Two smaller companies had been circling the same deal, desperate to secure it and keep their businesses afloat. They had good teams and decent products, but not the edge that Asher had. And he knew it.

Instead of competing fairly, Asher pulled strings behind closed doors. He whispered in the right ears at the city commission office, made promises he didn't intend to keep, and secured exclusivity clauses that shut out the other companies entirely. By the time they realized what had happened, it was too late. Asher had the deal.

A year later, when the smaller companies were drowning, he swooped in with a clean offer: a buyout. Publicly, it looked like a lifeline. Privately, he knew it was a grave he had dug for them. He smiled for the cameras, shook hands with relieved employees, and told his father and Aunt Robin that it was an expansion, a brilliant strategy for growth.

"It was a clean transaction," he told them over dinner one Sunday, pushing his glass of water aside and cutting neatly into a steak. "They needed a way out. We gave them stability, and in return, we doubled our capacity. Everybody wins."

Keith had beamed at him, pride shining in his tired eyes. "That's my boy. Building something real. Building a legacy." Asher raised his glass, smiling back. He didn't correct him. He didn't admit that the "legacy" was built on deceit.

The memory shattered, yanked away by the groan of the hospital door. Keith's voice broke in as he stepped inside, his phone buzzing faintly in his hand. Carolina glanced up from the chair, her expression tight with fatigue.

"I've got to take this," Keith said, his voice low. He gestured with the phone. "It's Robin."

Carolina nodded, leaning back in her chair as he stepped toward the window. He pressed the phone to his ear, his back turned partly to her.

"Robin," he said, his voice softening instantly. "I'm glad you called."

Her voice crackled faintly from the other end, warm and familiar. "Keith, how is he?"

Keith pressed his palm against the glass of the window, his shoulders heavy. "No change. Still in a coma. The doctors… they don't say much, just that he's stable. Stable feels like a cruel word right now."

Robin's sigh traveled across the distance. "I wish I could be there. I've been trying to move our flight. I'll be back in four to five days at the latest."

"Four to Five days…" Keith repeated, his voice breaking faintly. "That feels like forever. You were there when Amelia went. You stepped in when everything fell apart. And now…" His words caught. "I can't do this again, Robin. I can't bury him either."

Robin's voice thickened with emotion. "Keith, listen to me. Asher is strong. You've always said it yourself. He carried that spark from the time he was a boy. Hold onto that. Don't let go yet."

Keith closed his eyes, nodding though she couldn't see him. "I'll try."

"I'll be there soon," Robin promised. "Stay strong for both of them. For Carolina, too."

The line buzzed softly before ending. Keith lowered the phone, his hand trembling as he slid it into his pocket. He turned back toward the bed, his eyes glassy.

"I'm stepping out for more air," he told Carolina, his voice hoarse. She only nodded, her hand brushing against her brother's.

Keith slipped out quietly, leaving the door ajar behind him.

Carolina sat a while longer before the stiffness in her body forced her up. She glanced at her brother one more time, her hand lingering on the edge of the bed. "Don't you dare leave me," she whispered, then straightened. "I'll be back. I need a break."

She stepped out into the hall, her footsteps soft against the tile as she headed toward the cafeteria. The door eased shut behind her.

The room was still. Late afternoon light streamed in through the blinds, casting angled bars across the blanket. The monitor kept its steady rhythm, indifferent to the storm inside his mind.

Asher drifted again.

Money had changed everything. With the acquisitions under his belt and his company growing faster than he could keep track, Asher found himself in a new orbit. Invitations to parties, black-tie events, investor dinners. People who once ignored him now called him by name.

At first, he bought little luxuries…. a nicer watch, tailored suits, and a sleek car that hummed like a secret when he pressed the accelerator. But soon, "little" wasn't enough. He wanted more. More shine, more speed, more rooms where people turned their heads when he walked in.

The casinos came next.

It started small. A trip with business partners after a successful pitch, just a few chips on the table. He laughed when he lost, bought another round, and told himself it was harmless. But harmless turned to hunger. Hunger had turned to habit.

Soon he was flying out on weekends, slipping into dimly lit rooms with velvet carpets and where cards hit the table that felt like thunder. The dealers smiled, the servers kept his glass full, and the rush filled the hollow spaces he never wanted to name.

The first time he won big … five figures on the turn of a card, he felt invincible. He threw bills onto the bar, bought drinks for strangers, tipped until people clapped him on the back and called him generous.

But the losses followed. Quiet at first, then louder. He kept playing, chasing the high of the win.

One night, he sat in a private room, the table crowded with men in suits heavier than his, their eyes sharp, their smiles thin. His chips dwindled, but he laughed, pretending it was just a game. Inside, though, he felt the gnaw of desperation.

He thought of Carolina that night. The promise he had made her after the first DUI. No more drinking. No more recklessness.

Her face flickered in his mind as he raised his hand for another card.

"She won't find out," he muttered under his breath, forcing the thought away.

The dealer slid the card across the table. Asher swallowed hard, staring at it, the weight of his own lie heavy in his chest.

Afterward, when the casino lights blurred into morning haze, he numbed the shame with purchases. A second car, faster, sleeker. Another watch, gold catching the light. A wardrobe of suits tailored in cities he barely remembered visiting.

Every swipe of his card, every receipt tucked away, felt like a declaration: I'm winning. I'm still in control.

But deep down, he knew. Each purchase was a plastered smile over the cracks.

Back in the hospital room, his chest rose and fell, steady but shallow. The monitor beeped on, counting time the way no casino ever did.

Carolina's footsteps echoed faintly in the hall as she returned with a tray of cafeteria food. Keith's shadow stretched long in the corridor as he finished another slow lap of walking. Neither had any idea what worlds Asher was reliving behind his closed eyes.

The silence filled the room again, thick and unbroken. Keith returned to the room as the evening shadows lengthened across the floor. The blinds cut the dim light into narrow stripes that stretched over the bed, climbing slowly up the opposite wall. The hallway had quieted; visiting hours were winding down, and the hushed voices of nurses carried faintly from the station.

Carolina was back seated where she had been all day, now eating her turkey sandwich and potato chips with one hand resting lightly on the edge of Asher's blanket. Her eyes flicked up as her father came in, his steps heavy, his jacket folded loosely over his arm.

Neither spoke for a while. They sat together, letting the sounds of the machines fill the silence.

Finally, Keith rubbed his hand across his face, breaking the stillness. "I'll call Kramer in the morning," he said, his voice gravelly. "Maybe he'll have something new by then."

Carolina nodded slowly, her eyes locked on her brother. "I just don't understand," she whispered. "What could he have done? Who would want to hurt him like this?"

Keith let out a long, tired breath. He leaned forward, elbows on his knees, his hands clasped. "That's the mystery," he admitted. "And I want answers just as much as you do."

Carolina blinked hard, fighting the sting of tears. "I just… I keep thinking about Mom. About how helpless we felt then. And now it's happening again."

Keith reached across and placed his hand over hers. "This time, we'll stay strong together. No matter what we find out."

The weight of his words pressed into the room, settling between them like a pact, and neither dared to break.

They fell quiet again, the steady beeping of the monitor marking the slow passage of time. Keith leaned back in his chair, exhaustion etched deep in his face. Carolina rested her head lightly on her hand, her gaze never leaving her brother.

The room dimmed further as the evening gave way to the night. Outside, the city moved on, unaware of the silent vigil taking place inside the hospital walls.

Father and daughter sat quietly, both haunted by the same unanswered questions.

What did Asher get himself into?

And why would someone want to hurt him like this?

The questions lingered, heavy and unresolved, as Day One slipped quietly into darkness.

Chapter 8: The Ledger of Secrets

Morning crept into the hospital room in slow bands of light, pale and thin, stretching across the foot of Asher's bed. The overnight nurse finished her charting in the corner, the soft scrape of pen on paper almost soothing. Somewhere down the hall, a cart rattled, and the elevator chimed in neat, indifferent dings. The world outside was fully awake; inside, time moved at the pace of a heartbeat on a monitor.

Keith had risen before the sun, paced the length of the corridor, and returned with a paper cup of coffee he'd forgotten to drink. He stood now by the window, thumb worrying the rim of the lid, rehearsing the call he planned to make to the police station. He would be calm. He would be direct. He would ask for news and accept whatever they had to offer. Then he would sit down again beside his son and wait.

The door knocked twice, polite but firm, and swung open before Keith could say "come in."

Detective Kramer filled the doorway in a charcoal jacket, a folder tucked beneath one arm, his badge glinting briefly in the morning light. He nodded once to Keith, once to Carolina, then stepped in, easing the door shut behind him with the controlled quiet of a man who'd practiced entering rooms like this.

"Mr. Forest. Ms. Becker." His voice was steady, pitched low. "I hope I'm not too early."

Keith blinked, surprised. "I was just about to call your station."

"I thought I'd save you the trouble." Kramer shifted the folder to his other hand. Up close, the lines around his eyes looked deeper than last night, as if he'd slept less than either of them. "I have some updates, and I wanted you to hear them from me—not from a voicemail or a secondhand message."

Carolina stood from the chair, smoothing the front of her sweater with a nervous palm, and sat back down. "Is it about who did this?" Her gaze flicked to Asher, then back to the detective. "Did you find out who did this?"

"Not yet," Kramer said. "But we're tightening the picture around your brother's recent life. That helps us understand motive."

Keith moved to the foot of the bed, the coffee cup crumpling faintly in his grip. "Go on."

Kramer opened the folder. A thin stack of printed emails and typed notes lay clipped inside, a few business logos in color catching the light. "You told me your son expanded his company last year by acquiring two small firms. You said he described those deals as clean. Routine."

"That's what he told me," Keith said. "He said the owners were struggling, and he gave them a way out. It was business. An expansion."

Kramer tapped a finger against the top page. "We've spoken to the principals from both companies. Their account is… different. They allege that your son maneuvered behind the scenes to block their access to a key client. He secured an exclusivity clause first, effectively starving them of their largest potential contract. Once their runway shortened, he approached with a buyout offer."

Carolina's mouth parted, but no sound came. Keith set the coffee down on the tray, slowly, as if any sudden movement might fracture the air.

Kramer continued, voice even. "They claim he railroaded them. Their word. They wanted their companies back or compensation for damages. They say they were advised that no criminal charges would stick and that their recourse was civil court."

"Then they should've filed," Keith said, too quickly, the words tripping over each other. "If they really believed that they were railroaded, then they should have…"

"They didn't," Kramer said. "There's no record of a suit from either group."

"Why not?" Carolina asked, her voice was sharper than she had intended. "If what they're saying is true, why not file? Why tell you now?"

"That's the part I don't like," Kramer said. "Two detectives from my team are en route to meet with those owners this morning to answer exactly that question…. why they never pursued a civil case, and why they're talking now. I can't speculate yet. But the timing matters."

Keith's eyes darkened with something like hurt. He shook his head, slow and stubborn. "Asher told me it was clean. A clean transaction. He said he was expanding the business, bringing in good teams, saving jobs. He wouldn't….."

Kramer's tone didn't change. "Mr. Forest, I'm not here to pronounce judgment on your son's character. I'm here to assemble facts. Right now, some of those facts are in conflict."

Carolina blinked hard. "So, people think he ruined them," she said, half to herself. "They think he took their work and then took their names off the door."

Kramer gave a single, reluctant nod. "That's one set of statements, yes."

Keith pressed his palm over the blanket near Asher's shin, as if he could steady himself on the cotton. He looked at his son's face, slack with sleep that wasn't sleep, and said softly, "If that's true, then tell me why you didn't tell me, son. Why did you tell me it was clean when it wasn't?"

A silence opened, fragile and raw.

Kramer closed the folder but didn't tuck it away. "There's more," he said. "I've been making inquiries with local gaming establishments. Your son was a regular patron at two casinos within driving distance of each other. He's documented in security logs, host lists, and complimentary service records, dinners, rooms, and the usual amenities. According to preliminary statements, he has outstanding markers at both locations."

Carolina bristled, the heat rising up her neck like a rash. "Markers?"

"Lines of credit extended by the casino to favored players," Kramer said. "They function like short-term loans. High-dollar wagers are recorded against them."

Keith straightened, his voice brittle. "How much money are we talking about, Detective?"

Kramer's mouth pressed into a thin line. "Right now, what we can verify is in the tens to hundreds of thousands. That's the range I'm comfortable stating without documentation in hand. We're still working to confirm whether additional markers exist at larger, out-of-state properties."

"Tens to thousands," Keith stopped. "He… he runs a successful company. He has money. Why would he…" He cut himself off, like the act of asking the question made something more real.

"That's not true," Carolina said suddenly, a flare of anger igniting through the ache. "You're lying." The words came harsh and fast, sharper than she intended, but she didn't pull them back. "Asher didn't gamble. He bought things, yes; he liked nice suits, watches, and cars. But he didn't need to gamble. He had more than enough."

Kramer didn't flinch. "I understand your frustration," he said quietly. "Truly. None of this is easy to hear. But we're not guessing. We're collecting. Some hosts know him by name. There are records. There are debts. We're trying to determine if those debts connect to anything… larger."

Carolina's breath quickened. She pressed her knuckles to her mouth, eyes burning. "He promised me," she whispered. "He promised after…." The rest evaporated in her throat.

"Ms. Becker," Kramer said, gentler, "I'm not here to discredit your brother. People carry parts of themselves they don't show to family. That doesn't make them monsters. It makes them human. My job is to find out which hidden parts matter to this case."

Keith stared at Asher, his voice a rasp. "What is going on, son?"

The monitor answered with its patient's metronome, oblivious to human questions.

For a moment, no one said anything. Kramer let the silence stand, a space for the weight of the words to settle.

He checked his watch. "I'll return later today," he said. "Two of my detectives will report back after they meet with those former owners. I'm also waiting on a call from a compliance officer at one of the casinos."

"My hope" …. he let the word breathe, not promising…. "is that none of this ties to something deeper. But if it does, I'd rather find it now than later."

Keith rubbed the bridge of his nose, eyes closed, as if fending off a headache. "Find it," he said. "Whatever it is."

Kramer dipped his head. "We will." He glanced once more at Asher, a look without judgment. "I'm sorry you're having to hear this in pieces. I know that makes every hour longer." He turned for the door, paused with his hand on the handle.

"If either of you remembers anything…arguments, unfamiliar names, sudden changes in routine…call me. Even if it seems small."

He left as he'd come quietly, the door easing shut with a soft seal that changed the air pressure just enough to feel.

The room absorbed him. Outside, someone laughed too brightly at something in the hall. A cart squeaked by. Keith didn't move. Carolina sank back into the chair like the springs beneath her had gone out.

"He's wrong," she said, though her voice lacked conviction now. "He has to be."

Keith didn't answer. He stared at his son's hand, the way the veins ran faint beneath the skin, and thought of a thirteen-year-old boy in a basement lit by a square of electric blue, declaring he was building something. He thought of the graduation speech and the words 'clean' spoken as the truth. He thought of the detective's folder and the slow, careful way a man who trafficked in facts had said alleged and markers and range.

"I don't know," Keith said finally, not to contradict, not to concede, but because the truth was a shifting thing in his throat. "I just don't know."

Carolina folded herself forward, elbows on knees, forehead in her hands. "What did he get into?" she asked, the question small and enormous at once. "What could be so bad that someone…" She lifted her head, eyes flashing to Asher's bruised temple, then away. "Why would anyone want to hurt him like this?"

Keith didn't try to answer. He pulled a chair closer instead and sat, the metal legs whispering along the tile. He reached across the blanket and found his son's wrist, laying his fingers over the pulse point like a man counting rain. One… two… three… There it is. Proof of life that didn't respond to questions.

They let the minutes pass without speech. Morning thickened into something steadier. The shadow of the blinds crawled from the foot of the bed up across Asher's legs, over his chest, toward his shoulder.

A nurse slipped in and adjusted a line, murmuring the sort of encouragement in the room's direction that people offer because they need to throw their hope somewhere. She looked at Carolina before she left. "You should try to eat," she said. "There's oatmeal in the cafeteria that's almost passable."

Carolina managed a half-smile that didn't hold. "I will. In a bit."

When the door closed again, Keith drew a breath as if surfacing. "I'm going to call Robin," he said. "Give her the update before she hears any of it from someone else."

Carolina nodded, rubbing her palms together to warm the chill that hospital air always carried. "Tell her I love her."

He stepped into the hall to make the call, the door falling softly shut behind him. Through the glass panel, Carolina could see the blur of his form as he lifted the phone to his ear and began to pace in a tight, contained loop.

She stood and stretched, her muscles protesting. The room smelled faintly of antiseptic and whatever the last person to walk through had carried with them. She leaned over Asher. "I'll be right back," she whispered, as if he might decide to wake at the exact moment she left. "Don't do anything without me."

The hallway was busier now, with orderlies carrying trays, a volunteer with a basket of magazines, and the tired choreography of morning after a hard night. Carolina followed the line of arrows on the floor toward the cafeteria, more to get away from the walls than to eat. She promised herself she would return in ten minutes. Fifteen, at most. As if keeping that small promise might balance the ledger of all the promises that had already been broken in this family.

Back in the room, the hush asserted itself, claiming the corners and the spaces under the machines. Asher lay exactly where they left him, one arm outside the blanket, the tape on his wrist neat and unruffled. The monitor counted, the drip whispered, the blinds cast their uneven bars.

Inside his mind, the door that had opened to greed's first bite lifted again to a darker room.

He saw tables under flat light, the green of them soft and merciless. He smelled cologne and the burnt-sugar bitterness of an old-fashioned. He heard the shush of cards dealt with a dealer's practiced indifference and the crisp rattle of chips sliding into the center. Names floated at the edge of his memory: hosts who greeted him like a friend, pit bosses who nodded, players who smiled without showing their teeth.

He saw a marker form slide towards him on a leather clipboard. He saw his own hand sign in a version of his name he used when he wanted to feel more certain of himself. He saw numbers written that, on paper, he could cover. He saw the swing, the big win that bought three suits and silence, the bigger loss that bloomed like a bruise under his shirt where no one could see.

He heard a voice…his own…say, She won't find out. He listened to another calmer, colder reply: 'It's only money.' He saw where those two voices met. He saw how easily only money became someone else's, and how quickly someone else's became someone's patience.

A shadow slipped through the memory like an ink spill. A man at the rail who watched more than he played. A name that wasn't a real name. A debt that stopped being a number and became an appointment.

Asher tried to turn from it, to find the bright basement screen and the clean code of his boyhood. The tables did not let him go. The door that led out was the same door that led deeper into the building.

In the waiting room, Keith ended his call and stood with his palm against the cool glass of the door, gathering himself before he re-entered. Down the hall, Carolina waited in front of a vending machine longer than any person needed to decide between bottled water and juice.

The morning settled. The detective's card sat like a small white flag atop the folder, waiting.

When Carolina returned with a honey bun and a bottle of orange juice, Keith had retaken his seat. They nodded to each other, that wordless language people in crisis master, and chose, for the moment, not to speak of markers or hostile acquisitions. They sat and listened to the monitor, pretending that the sound held more significance than it actually did.

Kramer's updates hung in the air like a draft you can't locate… present, just cold enough to raise gooseflesh.

Keith reached for his son's hand. "Whatever this is," he said under his breath, words meant for ears that might or might not hear, "we'll face it. But you have to wake up to do it."

The blinds carved the light into narrower bands. The clock shifted past another hour. Somewhere, the phone rang twice and stopped.

Inside Asher's drifting dark, the table brightened again, and the shadow at the rail stepped closer. The debt began to speak in a voice that didn't need to raise itself to be heard.

And the day moved on.

Chapter 9: The Breaking Point

The clock ticked past noon, its steady rhythm competing with the pulse of the monitors. Carolina shifted in her chair, her eyes stinging from hours of staring at her brother. She rubbed at her temples, knowing she needed to step away, if only for a little while.

Keith caught her restless glance and sighed. "Go home, sweetheart. Get a shower. Change your clothes. I'll stay until you get back, then I'll take my turn. We can't run ourselves down, not when he needs us steady."

Carolina hesitated. "I don't want to leave him alone."

"He won't be," Keith said firmly. "I'll be right here. You need a break. Trust me, I do too, but one of us has to stay."

Her shoulders sagged. She leaned over and brushed her fingers against Asher's hand. "I'll be back soon, Ash. Don't… don't do anything while I'm gone." The words sounded foolish, but they slipped out anyway, a ritual between siblings.

She grabbed her purse and walked out into the hallway, the door clicking closed behind her.

As she stepped into the air outside the hospital, it was sharp, cooler than she expected, and for the first time in hours, Carolina felt the weight of sunlight. It seemed wrong that the sky was so clear while her world had tilted into gray.

She slid into her car, started the engine, and let the radio hum to life before snapping it off again. Silence filled the interior, so thick it felt alive. Her hands gripped the steering wheel, knuckles pale, as she pulled onto the road. The city blurred around her… traffic lights changing, people walking with coffees in hand, a jogger pacing the sidewalk. All of it carried on as if nothing had happened. As if her brother wasn't lying in a hospital bed with bruises on his face and a machine counting each breath.

Carolina swallowed hard, her throat raw. The longer she drove, the more the silence pressed against her. Thoughts circled in sharp loops, cutting deeper each time.

What life were you living, Asher? Who did you become when we weren't looking?

The detective's words echoed: "Maybe he had secrets."

She clenched her jaw and pressed harder on the gas.

By the time she pulled into her driveway, her chest was tight, her breathing shallow. She barely remembered the last few turns, the automatic motions of pulling into her garage.

She killed the engine and stumbled out, fumbling with the keys, her body moving faster than her mind. She dropped her bag on the kitchen counter and went straight to the bathroom, stripping as she went.

The water in the shower was scalding when it hit her skin, but she didn't adjust it. She pressed her palms flat against the tile, her forehead bowed against the cool wall and let the water pound down her back.

The first sob tore out of her before she could stop it. Then another. Then a scream, raw and sharp, that echoed against the tiles.

She didn't care if the neighbors heard. She didn't care if the whole block heard. She screamed again, years of held breath pouring out of her, grief mixing with rage.

The sound became jagged, fractured, until her voice broke into hoarse sobs. She sank to her knees, the water rushing over her shoulders, her hair plastered to her face. She cried until the steam blurred everything and her skin burned.

Her fists pounded against her thighs. "Why, Asher? Why didn't you tell me? What were you doing behind closed doors?"

Her words cracked and fell apart in the spray.

She stayed like that until the water ran lukewarm.

Deep in thought, Carolina shut off the water and wrapped herself in a towel, her body trembling with exhaustion. She wiped a circle clear on the mirror, only to see her swollen eyes, her blotched skin. She barely recognized herself.

She sat on the closed lid of the toilet, the towel tucked tight around her and stared at the tiles. Her voice was quieter now, but the questions still clawed at her throat.

Do I even know who my brother really is? Or did I only know the version he wanted me to see?

She thought back to childhood, running through sprinklers, sharing secrets under the covers when storms rattled the windows, fighting over the last piece of pizza. She thought of the night he swore to her after the DUI, his eyes wide and desperate, promising change.

Was that a lie, too?

The thought made her stomach turn. She pressed a hand against her chest, trying to steady herself.

"I just want you back," she whispered. "Even if you're not who I thought you were… I want my brother back."

The words dissolved in the quiet.

Back at the hospital, Keith sat slumped in the chair beside his son's bed. The morning had stretched into afternoon, and fatigue pressed against his eyelids. He had called Robin again, to hear her voice, and told her the same thing he had before: there was no change.

Now, he sat in silence, the detective's words replaying in his head. Railroading. Gambling. Debts.

He rubbed a hand over his face, his stubble scratching against his palm. He wanted to reject it outright, to defend his son against every accusation. But fragments of memory slipped through, the way Asher's phone was constantly buzzing at dinner, the way his eyes sometimes flicked away when Keith asked a direct question.

Keith reached out and clasped Asher's hand, squeezing it tight. "If you're hiding something, son, I wish you'd told me. I could've helped. I would've helped." His voice broke. "But I can't fight shadows. I need you to wake up."

The monitor beeped steadily and indifferently.

Keith leaned back in his chair and closed his eyes, exhaustion tugging at him. His hand remained on his son's, as if letting go would mean losing him entirely.

By late afternoon, Carolina returned, her hair damp, her clothes fresh, her face paler but calmer. She carried a small bag with a sweater and a book she knew she wouldn't read.

Keith looked up as she entered. "Better?"

She gave a slight nod. "Not really. But cleaner."

He stood slowly, stretching the stiffness out of his back. "Then it's my turn. I'll go home, grab a shower, and change my clothes. I'll be back before nightfall."

Carolina set her bag down and moved to the chair he had vacated. "I'll stay with him."

Keith placed a hand on her shoulder, a gentle squeeze of solidarity. "We'll figure this out," he said quietly. "One way or another, we'll find out what he got tangled in."

Carolina swallowed and nodded, but the words she wanted to say stayed lodged in her throat. What if I don't want to know?

Keith grabbed his jacket and left, the door clicking shut behind him.

Carolina sat, her hand finding her brother's once more. She leaned forward, pressing her forehead against the back of his hand.

"Wake up, Asher," she whispered. "Even if you're not the man I thought you were… wake up and tell me the truth yourself."

The machines answered in their steady rhythm, but Asher remained still. Carolina sat in silence, her eyes fixed on her brother, her thoughts circling the same unyielding questions.

What life were you leading, Asher? What secrets did you keep? Do I even know you at all?

The room gave no answers. Only the steady, indifferent beat of the monitor carried through the quiet. Carolina pulled her bag closer and unzipped the front pocket. From inside, she slipped out a worn photograph… the four of them, back before loss reshaped everything. Her mother and father, Asher, who was smiling with his arm around their mother. Herself, a teenager with too much eyeliner. Asher, barely eleven, his grin still innocent, his eyes bright with a spark that no storm had dimmed.

She set the photo gently on the bedside table, sliding it just close enough so that it leaned against the base of the lamp, angled toward Asher.

For a long moment, she studied it, her chest tightening until she couldn't hold the words back.

"You are my brother," she whispered, her voice trembling but steadying with each word. "Despite whatever you've gotten yourself into, we will get through it. Together."

Her fingers brushed the corner of the frame before she leaned back in her chair, eyes glistening, the photo standing as the machines hummed on.

And with that small vow, Day Two drew its curtain. And Asher's subconscious mind drifted.

Chapter 10: The Gentleman with the Open Hand

The room's hush folded into Asher's mind like a curtain drawn, and when it lifted, the world on the other side was velvet and light.

Cards. Felt. The soft percussion of chips stacking, breaking, and stacking again. A dealer's voice that never rose above calm. The air smelled like cologne and citrus and something sweet, the kind of sweetness that clung to your tongue and made you think of easy wins.

He was in a private room tonight, not the noisy main floor with its tourists and hopefuls. The door closed behind him with that expensive hush reserved for people who didn't like being overheard. The carpet drowned out the sound of footsteps. The table was round, the chairs deep, the lighting low and forgiving.

"Mr. Forest," the host said, smiling with the sort of memory that wasn't really memory so much as a note in a file. "Your table. Your game. Would you like your usual?"

"My usual," Asher said, and a glass appeared before he saw a hand move. He told himself he would only sip. He told himself a lot of things.

The first hour went like a story he'd told before, a light warm-up, just enough to remind the table his name wasn't new around here. A small win early to set the rhythm. A few losses he shrugged off to keep from inviting attention. His phone vibrated once in his jacket, and he didn't check it;

he knew it would be a message he could answer with 'Soon,' 'Tomorrow,' or 'Handled.'

He was up five figures by midnight. Not much in the scheme of what he now considered much, but enough to feel the old, narcotic hum wind through his bones.

He told himself he was calculating odds. What he was really measuring was momentum.

When the shoes changed and the deck felt colder, he stepped back, like a man who recognizes the first drops of rain and moves under an awning. Not a retreat. A pause. He knew how to wait for the weather to turn.

That was when Grayson Rivers's name was mentioned in the same breath as his own.

"Mr. Rivers wanted me to say hello," the host murmured, appearing with the quiet certainty of a magician. "He's a friend to the house. He noticed you've been playing well these last months."

Asher looked toward the smoked glass, where reflections failed to give up anything but silhouettes. "Mr. Rivers?" he said, as if the name were new to him. It wasn't. You didn't play the rooms he'd been playing and miss the rumor of Rivers: money moving under everything, current pulling those who stepped too close.

"If he can be of any assistance," the host went on, "he likes to support men who know how to make money behave."

Asher smiled without showing teeth. "I make money behave just fine."

"Of course," the host said, and his smile didn't shrink. "Still. If you prefer to keep your capital liquid for business, Mr. Rivers offers a… courtesy. He's generous. He also appreciates punctuality."

There it was, the first line of credit, dressed up like kindness. A handshake extended over a river that didn't look like a river.

"How punctual?" Asher said lightly.

"Very," the host murmured, and departed as if he'd changed the air.

The first time, Asher took Grayson's money. It felt like a test he was more than prepared to pass.

It was not a large sum, compared to what he carried in accounts labeled Operations, R&D, and Tax. It slid to him in a number written cleanly on a single sheet, the ink unfussy, the terms clear, short, direct, no interest if paid promptly, the sort of favor extended to a man whose reputation suggested the favor would be returned in triplicate.

Grayson didn't come to the table. He didn't have to. The house had a way of making its presence felt without a physical body, like the hint of current beneath a boat even on a windless day.

Asher accepted the marker as if it were a clever way to announce he understood leverage. Why tie up his own cash when someone else's wanted to work? He played with a steadier pulse than he had in months. He didn't chase. He waited for the deck to turn and stepped into the exact right moment like a man timing a jump onto a moving train.

He won. Handsome, smooth, the kind of win that makes a dealer blink. He paid Grayson back in full before the sun had risen on the city, the number gone as cleanly as it had arrived. The host conveyed Mr. Rivers' compliments in the afternoon.

"Efficient," the message said. "I appreciate working with efficient men."

It felt good. Too good. Like a secret handshake into a club that prided itself on not using the word club.

The second loan came easier, almost offhand. Another night, another table, momentum at his back. He hadn't planned to extend himself; he liked the idea of playing on someone else's current, but he wanted even more the idea of not needing it. Still, the host materialized at his elbow with the knowing reserved for croupiers and confessors.

"Mr. Rivers sends his regards," he said, as if announcing a dessert course. "If you find yourself inclined."

Asher didn't need it. He took it anyway. The calculus was simple: keep his own cash where it could do the kind of work that got written up in tech journals and board minutes. Use other people's money for the adrenaline.

He told himself it wasn't greed. It was efficiency.

He played with Rivers' money a second time and won again more slowly, with a few long, cold stretches that would have made a lesser player blink. He didn't blink. He let the cold pass and stepped back in the second the air changed. Back in the suite, he wired the repayment himself, savoring the neatness of the transfer confirmation, just as he once admired clean, elegant code.

Grayson's reply came through the same mouthpiece as before: "You have a talent for timing."

The third loan was larger. Not obscene, but significant enough to require attention. It came on a night when the city outside felt electric, the kind of energy that kept him pacing the hotel room even after he'd run five miles and answered every message worth answering.

He told himself he was only going down to the floor to take a look. To stretch his legs. To be near a particular table where his breathing seemed a little better when the dealer spread cards.

He took a seat. He didn't plan to take the cards but told himself it was a warm-up. The warm-up turned into a hand-worth-pressing forward. When the host passed with a linen smile, Asher lifted two fingers without looking up. The clipboard arrived because, of course, the clipboard always arrived when summoned by men who played in these rooms.

He signed without a tremor. The first hour was a workout, sweatless and precise. The second hour asked for nerve. The third hour rewarded it with a series of small, relentless wins that weren't as sexy as one big swing, but which built a stack that made his forearms ache pleasantly. He paid the third loan, later than the first two, but still within the definition of punctuality that the house had taught him to adopt.

"Consistent," came the message, and he felt a childish flicker of pride that annoyed him the second it appeared.

With each repayment, something invisible shifted in the room. Not at the tables; he still played those like a man who understood the difference between heat and illusion. The shift lived in the orbit around him, a nod from a pit boss who'd never nodded before, a server who remembered his preference for a twist over a wedge. A chair always seemed to be available at the table he favored, even on nights when nothing was available for anyone. He told himself it was because he was winning. Another part of him understood the truth: houses take care of men who pay their markers quickly. It wasn't personal. It was arithmetic.

He started to believe he was special anyway.

Winning breeds a myth: that the table recognizes you, that dealers call the cards to your hand, that some unseen mechanism rewards your discipline like a god who loves men with neat spreadsheets. It was a flattering lie, and Asher had always been susceptible to the kind that came dressed as reason.

The fourth loan came on a night when everything seemed to be going in his favor. The city's IT Department had approved a pilot for one of his new civic dashboards. A regional partner had extended early purchase orders with terms he liked. The press had run a piece that used words like visionary and unflappable. He didn't believe his own press, not exactly, but he recognized that it was useful to let others do so.

He told himself he was there to celebrate. He told himself he would leave early.

The room felt familiar, which is the most dangerous kind of feeling in rooms like that. Familiarity lets you loosen a button you shouldn't, ignore a draft you should, call a number higher than you planned because the last three numbers behaved gently.

"Mr. Rivers sends his compliments," the host said, as if speaking a ritual. "And his courtesy, should you wish it."

Asher should have said no. Not because he couldn't cover it, he could, at least on paper, but because something in him recognized that the number the host named was not like the numbers before it. It wasn't just larger. It asked for a different kind of nerve. It assumed a different kind of certainty.

He paused long enough to hear the hesitation. Then he signed anyway.

The first hand was a lesson in humility dressed as patience. He folded when he would normally ride. He watched the table breathe and waited for the moment when the dealer's movements shifted a fraction faster, a fraction looser. He pressed then, but the table rolled its indifferent shoulder and let him slide off.

He told himself a simple story of variance. No system is perfect, the long game pays. The long game will pay.

He lost, hands that should not have been losses, hands that slipped out of his fingers like a glass catching an elbow.

He adjusted. He changed his pace. He shortened his bets to keep blood moving to the right muscles. The table offered him a small win, like a dog that gives up a stick before tearing after it again, and he took it because men who survive these rooms know how to take what they're offered. He told himself the tide was turning. It wasn't. The tide had flattened long enough to let him step forward into deeper water.

An hour later, his stack looked like it had been chewed by something with efficient teeth.

He found a groove three hands, clean and elegant, with outcomes so textbook that they would look staged if written out in a thread. He pressed on the fourth. The fourth turned its face to the ceiling and took its breath with it.

He laughed then, quietly, because laughter is cheaper than panic and plays better in a room where men watch each other more than they watch the cards. He asked for water. He took a slow swallow. He wiped his mouth with the back of his hand in a gesture he knew read as reset.

The dealer's eyes were kind, which is to say they were blank. The kindness of a dealer is that there is no kindness—just mechanics.

He played to even. He played to survive. He played like a man who knew he should stand up, stretch, count the air in his lungs, and say goodnight.

He didn't stand up.

By the time he did, the number on the clipboard was larger than it had been when he sat down, and the room looked different. Not because the light had changed. Not because the people had. Because he had.

He signed the slip that acknowledged what he owed with the same clean hand he used to sign contracts that moved software across a skyline of bureaucracies. A host took the paper and smiled and said he hoped Mr. Forest had a good night.

Asher walked to the elevator with steps that felt normal. He looked at his reflection in the gold of the door and practiced a calm he had once created for investor calls, measured, inevitable. In the suite, he loosened his tie, took off his watch, and looked out at the slice of river that cut the city in two. He told himself a truth that had always served him well: I can outpace this.

He listed the ways while brushing his teeth. Another municipal contract: he had three proposals in final review; the city manager loved a dashboard that made a mess look as clean as a state-level pilot. A corporate client is due to renew at a higher tier because their team had integrated his software so tightly that removing it would feel like pulling out a spine.

Money was a network of arteries. He knew how to reroute blood.

He'd taken Grayson's courtesy because it was elegant to keep his own cash at work. He could pay him back with a portion of any of those incoming flows. He could accelerate receivables. He could trim a bonus cycle. He could call his CFO and sound grave and responsible, discussing "responsibility in a tighter quarter." He could sell a sliver of something that would grow back.

It's only money, he told himself, and the part of him that knew better nodded like a friend humoring a lie said for comfort.

He slept shallowly, every turn of the sheets a negotiation with the numbers lined up behind his eyes.

In the morning, his phone chimed with three meetings he had to attend, two of which he could cancel, and one he wanted to participate in. He canceled the two. He took the one. He returned one missed call from a number he knew not to save and received a voice so smooth he could almost pour it over ice.

"Mr. Forest," the voice said. No need for names. "Always a pleasure."

"I'll have you squared by the end of the week," Asher said crisply. "Invoices are clearing, and a contract closing. I'll wire when the ink is dry."

"Of course," the voice said, as if they were discussing a tee time. "Punctuality keeps friendships friendly."

"It won't be a problem," Asher said, and meant it. In that hour. With that coffee. The city appears to be a grid of solvable problems.

A day passed. Two. The contract had shifted by a week because a procurement officer went on leave. The invoices cleared at a pace that was both standard and intolerable. His CFO asked a question about cash positioning that he deflected with a sentence that said everything and nothing. He moved a meeting. He made it sound like a strategy.

The call came again. Same number. Same temperature.

"As expected," Asher said before the voice could speak. "End of the week became Monday. The city's calendar is a glacier. But movement is movement. We're good."

"Glad to hear it," the voice said. "We enjoy good."

He wired what he could that Monday, a substantial amount that put a visible dent in the number, which still looked like a wall. He didn't love the feeling. He didn't love the way making a dent didn't feel like progress so much as confirmation that the wall was real.

The second call after that one did not ask for anything. It congratulated him on the partial and told him the house appreciated the relationship.

Two nights later, he went back.

He told himself he would play smart. He told himself there would be no clipboard.

There was a clipboard.

He took it without looking down like a man who has done a thing enough times to believe it isn't a choice. The number this time was not simply higher; it was configured to demand a narrative. Men who borrowed at that figure told themselves they had a plan. Plans erase fear. Plans are the narcotic that lets numbers grow without pain.

He lost. Not theatrically. Not in a way that would rile a table. Piece by piece, the way a shoreline changes if you stare at it long enough, nothing dramatic to point to, except for the total at the end.

He said the line that had worked for years: I'll outpace it. He added a new one, he meant with a ferocity that surprised him: I'll sell something. If I have to, I'll sell something.

He enumerated the assets that, on paper, were liquid. He ignored the ones that were not.

He did not panic. He did not let himself live in that world. He lived instead in the familiar: I know how to multiply money. I always have. Give me a quarter, and I'll give you a dollar. Give me a year, and I'll give you a system. Give me a problem, and I'll build the thing that solves it.

He took a shower that ran too hot and stood under it too long, the way men do when they need to feel something physical they can control. He dressed in a suit that told better stories than his face did. He smiled at a mirror that didn't argue.

He wired another partial, the partial that would reassure a man who dealt in arithmetic.

The reply came swiftly, almost warmly. We see your effort. Keep the tempo.

Tempo. He liked the word. It allowed him to pretend he was conducting something, rather than being conducted.

He did not tell Carolina. He did not tell his father. He did not tell Aunt Robin. He told his COO they'd reprioritized spend because of an "unexpected municipal window." He told himself that nothing he said was technically untrue. Half-truths were cheaper than lies and easier to carry.

He built a new projection spreadsheet at midnight, with tabs labeled with clean nouns: Bridge. Ramp. Pivot. He reassured himself that naming things gave them borders.

At the edge of the sheet, where the numbers belonging to the tables sat in their own column, he added a line that read 'R courtesy.' Courtesy, as if the money had tipped its hat when it crossed the line into his hand.

Next week, another call. Another voice with the same temperature. An invitation phrased like an observation. "The room misses you."

Rooms do not miss men, but men who miss rooms believe they do.

He went. Of course, he went. He told himself he would sit, watch, let the air inform him, and leave. He sat. He watched. He played.

He found a groove that might have redeemed the previous slip. He pressed. The groove swerved. The table looked at him the way tables do when they've won without effort.

He stood up, nodded toward the dealer, shook the host's hand, and said the kind of sentence a man says when he wants other men to think he is unaffected. "Another night."

He wasn't affected. He also wasn't undone. He had been in tighter corners. He had built himself out of worse situations…. he told himself, thinking of other nights, other kinds of darker nights.

On the street outside, the city smelled like rain that wasn't there yet. He breathed like a man who believed air could be a strategy.

He pulled his phone out and typed a short message to a man in the city who owed him a favor. He typed another to a private buyer about a module that would not weaken his platform if he parted with it. He drafted an email to his CFO about adjusting burn to "respect the quarter's shape." He did not hit send on any of them. He held them there, little digital promises lined up like pills he could take if the headache grew.

Back in the suite, he opened the curtains and looked at the dark like it had answers. He felt calm. Or he chose to call what he felt calm.

He lay down and told himself the thing he had told himself after he failed his exam and still built a company, after he went too far and still talked his way back, after every loss that could be framed as a prelude.

I never stay down.

In the hospital room, a monitor made the noise it always makes when nothing changes. The blinds striped the bed in the morning that wasn't morning, day that wasn't day. A photo leaned against the lamp base of a father, a mother, a daughter, a son, all looking into a camera that could not know what time would do.

Carolina dozed in the chair, her head tilted toward her brother's hand. Keith's footsteps were a rumor down the hall, his return measured in the soft cadence of a man who had remembered where the floor squeaks.

Inside Asher's mind, the gentleman with an open hand smiled with generosity and spoke with patience and kept impeccable records.

Asher told himself, again, that he would outpace him.

He told himself that selling one more thing would set the ledger right.

He told himself that he had time.

And the door to the velvet room stayed open, the air inside exactly the temperature he preferred.

Chapter 11: The Weight of Numbers

The third day in the hospital began the way the second had ended: with the sound of machines. The rhythmic beeping, the soft hiss of oxygen, the shuffle of nurses on rounds. The blinds were tilted half open, letting in the thin gray light of a city morning.

Keith sat at the foot of Asher's bed, his shoulders rounded, the wrinkles at the corners of his eyes deeper than they had been a week ago. Carolina stirred her coffee cup mechanically, the contents already cold, her gaze fixed on the rise and fall of her brother's chest.

Neither had slept much. Sleep in hospitals was a fragile, broken thing, chairs that never reclined enough, interruptions that came at the worst times, and the weight of waiting that pressed down harder than exhaustion.

Carolina finally set her cup aside with a sigh. "Another day," she murmured. "Another day of nothing."

Keith rubbed his temples. "Another day of hoping."

The knock came soft but deliberate. Both looked up as the door swung open and Detective Kramer stepped inside. His jacket was darker today, his shirt freshly pressed, but his eyes betrayed the hours he'd been keeping. He carried a thick folder under his arm, one that seemed heavier than the one he had before.

"Good morning," Kramer said evenly. "I hope I'm not intruding."

Keith straightened in his chair, tension winding through his frame. "We were expecting your call. Not your visit."

"I thought it best to come in person," Kramer said, moving closer. He rested the folder on the tray table at the foot of the bed and sat down in the empty chair. "I have some updates."

Carolina crossed her arms, bracing herself. "What kind of updates?"

Kramer's expression gave nothing away, but the pause before he opened the folder made both of them stiffen. He flipped it open; the pages were crisp and clipped together in neat sections. Kramar rested his notebook on his knee, his tone even but clipped. "There's something else we followed up on. Early on, we had questions about why the two business owners never filed lawsuits against your son. I spoke with them personally. "One of them wouldn't give me a straight answer. All he said was that he had changed his mind, and then he shut the door on further questions. The other admitted he was advised not to file, but when I pressed him for details, he clammed up. Wouldn't say another word. Both of them made it clear they weren't interested in revisiting the matter."

He flipped a page, the scratch of his pen the only sound in the room. "So that trail, at least for now…is a dead end."

Keith and Carolina exchanged a look, a flicker of relief passing between them. For all the uncertainty still pressing in, this was one corner they no longer had to fear collapsing.

Kramar didn't let the pause stretch long. "We've confirmed some things about your brother's financial activity," he said. "Specifically, his gambling habits." Keith's hand clenched around the arm of his chair. "We already discussed this yesterday. Casinos, markers. You said you were checking into it."

"I was," Kramer said. "And now I have clearer numbers." Kramar rested his hands on the back of an empty chair, voice steady but measured.

"We've learned that Asher borrowed money tied to the casino. At first, he repaid it quickly and cleanly. But over time, the debt grew. And the people he borrowed from… they don't operate like the casinos. They extend credit off the books. High rollers who want bigger hands than the house will cover, they make it happen for a price. And when payments slip, the consequences aren't just financial."

Carolina's face hardened. "A loan shark?"

Kramar's mouth twitched, not quite a smile. "That's one way to put it. Officially, these are businessmen with investments in private ventures. Unofficially, they make their living keeping people hooked and paying. Keith shook his head. "My son doesn't…he wouldn't"

Kramer raised his hand gently. "Mr. Forest, I'm not asking you to believe or defend. I'm telling you what's been verified. Your son accepted three loans. He paid the first three back. Cleanly."

"Then what's the problem?" Keith demanded, as if the neat repayments could erase the implication.

Kramer's eyes rested on him, steady. "The problem is the fourth loan."

The silence that followed was heavier than the machines, thicker than the walls. Carolina swallowed, her throat dry. "How much?"

Kramer took a breath before answering. "Four and a half million dollars."

Carolina's mouth fell open, but no sound came. Keith leaned back as if struck, his lips parting around words that wouldn't form.

"Four point five," Keith finally stammered. "That's… that's impossible. That's not gambling. That's madness."

"It's high-stakes gambling," Kramar said, his tone measured. "And it's documented. The casinos confirmed the markers, and our detectives confirmed the loans."

Carolina shot to her feet, her voice breaking. "You're lying. You have to be. Asher didn't gamble like that. He wouldn't throw money away like that! He worked too hard for it." Kramar didn't flinch. "Ms. Becker, I understand how hard this is to hear. But the evidence doesn't bend for our feelings. Your brother was a high roller. And he had a financier who kept extending him credit when the casinos wouldn't."

Carolina's hands shook as she pointed toward the bed. "That's my brother. He built a company from nothing.

He put himself through school. He doesn't need a financier, or loans, or casinos."

"Maybe he didn't need them," Kramer said softly. "But he took them. And he lost."

Keith dragged both hands down his face, his jaw trembling with the effort to keep his composure. "Why?" he whispered. "Why would he dig himself into something like this?"

"That," Kramar said, closing the folder, "Is what we're working to determine. My team has reviewed the financial records, and one outstanding obligation remains unaccounted for. In this world, numbers like that aren't just money. It's pressure. It's motive."

Keith turned sharply. "Motive?"

"For why someone might want to send a message," Kramar said carefully. "Your son's beating may not have been random. It may have been a debt coming due."

Carolina covered her mouth, eyes welling. She turned toward her brother, her tears spilling freely. "No… no, Ash. What did you do?"

Keith's voice cracked, his hand gripping the bed rail. "Son, what is going on?"

The monitor beeped on, steady, indifferent, as if mocking their pleas.

Kramer slipped his papers back into the folder, his expression grim. "I don't share this to wound you. I share it because the truth helps us. Even the parts we'd rather not know."

Keith looked up sharply, anger in his eyes. "Truth? Or speculation?"

"Truth," Kramer said firmly. "Markers don't lie. Transactions don't disappear. The money was borrowed. The repayments were made. And now, four and a half million remains unresolved."

Carolina sobbed, pressing her fists against her eyes. "Why didn't he tell us? Why didn't he tell me?"

Keith's shoulders sagged, his pride hollowing into despair. "Because he knew we'd stop him."

The room fell silent except for Carolina's muffled cries and the endless rhythm of the machines. Finally, Kramar stood, tucking the folder under his arm. "I'll be speaking with a party connected to these transactions first thing in the morning. I want to hear their account and why three repayments passed without issue before this fourth one went sour."

Keith's jaw tightened. "And if you can't get in touch with them?"

Kramer's eyes flickered. "Then we'll keep pressing. One way or another, we'll find out how deep this river runs." He paused at the door, lowering his voice. "One more thing, you should be aware. The park's security cameras were offline that night, caught in the middle of a software update. They didn't record a thing. As for the street cameras, we did catch a black SUV turning into the park entrance, but the plates were missing. We're working to gather more information about the vehicle and whoever was inside."

His gaze lingered on Keith and Carolina, steady and deliberate. "I'll keep you updated. Every step."

Kramer gave them a final nod and left the room, his footsteps fading down the corridor until the hush closed in again.

Keith and Carolina sat in silence, staring at Asher's unmoving body. The monitor kept its indifferent rhythm, but it now felt louder, a reminder that life went on while truth gnawed at the edges of their hope.

Keith finally spoke, his voice low, cracked. "Four and a half million. My son? How could he…" His words trailed off, swallowed by the sterile air.

Carolina pressed her hands together, trembling. "I don't know who he is anymore."

They couldn't bear the silence a moment longer. Wordlessly, they rose together and slipped out of the room, their footsteps heavy down the hallway until they reached the hospital's main doors.

Outside, the air was brisk, sharp enough to sting their lungs. The world beyond the glass was moving as if nothing had changed …. cars passing, people entering and leaving, voices echoing faintly.

Keith let out a guttural sound and swung his fists into the air, punching at nothing, his body jerking forward as though he could strike the invisible weight crushing him.

"Damn it, Asher!" he shouted, his voice cracking, chest heaving. "What did you do?"

Carolina, unable to hold herself up, collapsed to her knees on the concrete steps. Her sobs tore through the air, raw and broken. She buried her face in her hands, the grief spilling from her like water finally breaching a dam.

A woman walking into the hospital stopped short, startled. She crouched near Carolina, concern etched on her face. "Are you okay?" she asked gently, reaching out a tentative hand.

Keith rushed over, pulling Carolina into his arms protectively before the woman could touch her. His eyes were fierce, his voice tight but controlled. "She's fine," he said quickly. "She just… needs a moment."

The bystander hesitated, glanced between them, then nodded awkwardly and moved inside, leaving them to their storm.

Keith held his daughter as she shook in his arms, both of them unraveling under the weight of lies they couldn't untangle, debts they couldn't explain, and a beating they couldn't understand. Neither dared say the truth out loud. Not here. Not to anyone else.

Carolina gasped through her sobs. "Dad… what if we never really knew him?"

Keith closed his eyes, pressing his jaw into her hair. His voice was hoarse, broken. "Then God help us both."

But in the shadows of his subconscious, Asher wasn't worried.

The debts were numbers. Nothing more. Numbers bent, always had. He had bent them before contracts, codes, and deals were made on tight deadlines. He was the man who turned problems into profits. Three loans taken. Three loans repaid. Clean. Efficient. The fourth? A temporary snag, a stumble he would erase with the next big win.

The money wasn't a chain. It was fuel. And Asher thrived on fuel. Each time the marker slid across the table, it was as if the room itself acknowledged his brilliance. He paid them back because that's what men like him did…they outpaced the world.

"I'll outpace it," he muttered in the recesses of his drifting mind. The words rang like a vow. "I'll sell another program. Land another city contract. Make another million before the ink dries."

He could see himself at the tables again, chips stacked, cards sliding his way, the dealer's expression unreadable. Losses didn't matter. They were setups, preludes to the comeback that always came.

He told himself the lie once more: I am invincible. I am untouchable.

And in the silence between heartbeats, the lie almost sounded like the truth.

Chapter 12: The Gentleman's Office

Detective Daniel Kramer had walked into plenty of places where the veneer of success was paper-thin: dusty storefronts with "For Lease" signs curled in the windows, back rooms that stank of smoke and fear, garages with greasy floors and half-broken locks.

This was not one of them.

The office tower in the heart of the financial district gleamed like a monument to legitimacy. Its glass façade mirrored the morning sky, every line sharp, every surface polished. Inside, the lobby glowed with marble floors, high ceilings, and a security desk staffed by men in tailored suits instead of uniforms. Everything about the place screamed credibility, confidence, and control.

Kramer checked in at the front desk, flashing his badge without ceremony. The guard made a quick call, then gestured for him to follow toward the elevators. "Fourteenth floor, Rivers Capital Group. They're expecting you."

The detective pressed the button, and the elevator rose in silence, its jazz music playing faintly from hidden speakers. He studied his reflection in the mirrored walls, the plain gray suit, the faint crease in his tie, the sharpness in his eyes that no amount of polish could smooth away.

When the doors slid open, he stepped into a reception area that looked more like a boutique hotel than a business office. A long walnut desk curved gracefully across the entry, behind which a poised receptionist greeted him with a professional smile. Her hair was pinned neatly, her blouse crisp, her voice warm.

"Detective Kramer," she said. "Mr. Rivers will see you shortly. Please, have a seat."

She gestured toward a cluster of leather chairs arranged around a glass coffee table. Magazines sat neatly fanned across the surface of business journals, not a hint of the tabloids or gossip rags. Phones rang quietly behind her, assistants moved briskly through glass-walled corridors, and the faint hum of printers and keyboards lent the air the soft industriousness of a company that thrived in daylight.

It would have fooled anyone else.

But Kramer knew better. Places like this worked harder to look clean because they had more to hide.

A young assistant in a navy suit appeared moments later. "Detective? Mr. Rivers will see you now."

Kramer followed him down a hallway lined with framed photographs of charity galas, ribbon cuttings, and awards from city officials. Grayson Rivers shook hands with governors, stood beside athletes, and smiled with mayors. The man was stitched into the fabric of the city's power.

The assistant opened a set of double doors, ushering Kramer inside.

Grayson Rivers rose from behind a broad walnut desk, the skyline spilling wide behind him through floor-to-ceiling windows. He was in his early fifties, tall and trim, his salt-and-pepper hair combed with meticulous precision. His suit was navy, the cut sharp, the cufflinks understated but expensive. He moved with the calm assurance of a man who never needed to raise his voice to be obeyed.

"Detective Kramer," he said smoothly, extending his hand. "Welcome. Always an honor to assist law enforcement."

Kramer clasped his hand, noting the firm grip, the practiced warmth in the smile. "Mr. Rivers. Thank you for taking the time."

"Please, have a seat," Rivers said, gesturing to the pair of leather chairs across from his desk. "Would you like a coffee? Tea? We keep a full bar, though it may be a bit early." His laugh was soft and disarming.

"I'll pass," Kramer said, lowering himself into the chair. "I won't keep you long. I'm here regarding Asher Forest."

The name landed like a pebble in still water.

For the briefest moment, Rivers froze. His pen, which he had been tapping lightly against a pad …stilled. His eyes flickered, betraying a shock too quickly to mask.

"Asher Forest," he repeated slowly, setting the pen down. "That's… unexpected. I haven't heard that name in some time. What about him?"

"He's alive," Kramer said evenly, watching him closely. "Barely. He's in the hospital. Beaten badly. In a coma."

Rivers blinked, his jaw tightening ever so slightly. He recovered quickly, but not quickly enough to hide the flash of surprise. "My God," he said softly. "That's… terrible. I had no idea."

Kramer leaned forward. "You didn't know he was in trouble?"

Rivers shook his head, his expression composed again, only the faintest crease between his brows betraying him. "Detective, I knew Mr. Forest socially, through certain business interests. He was young, brilliant, and ambitious. But no, I did not know of this… tragedy."

Kramer opened his notebook, flipping a page. "I'll be direct, Mr. Rivers. Asher's financial records tie back to companies under your control. Four loans. Three cleared. One amount is still outstanding, at $4.5 million. That's not pocket change. That's leverage."

Rivers folded his hands on the desk, his expression calm, voice measured. "Yes. That is correct."

The admission was so casual it startled Kramer. Rivers leaned back in his chair, speaking as if explaining a routine contract.

"Asher came to me over a year ago. Not because he was desperate, but because he was clever. The casinos cap their credit. Asher wanted to play larger than they allowed. He convinced me he had the means to cover it. And he did. Three times, he proved himself. Paid me back promptly. Efficiently. I respect that kind of man."

"Until the fourth time," Kramer said.

Rivers gave a slight shrug. "Until the fourth. He overextended. It happens. Men who win often begin to believe they always will."

"You extended him four and a half million," Kramer pressed. "Why so much?"

Rivers smiled thinly. "Because he asked for it. And because he convinced me he could handle it. I don't throw money at fools, Detective. Asher wasn't a fool. He was a visionary. Visionaries sometimes gamble bigger than the rest of us can stomach."

Kramer's pen scratched across the page. "And when visionaries fail? What happens then, Mr. Rivers?"

"Then we find solutions," Rivers replied smoothly. "Cash. Equity. Partnerships. There are always ways forward. Violence?" He shook his head. "That's bad for business."

"Tell me about the spiral," Kramer said.

Rivers steepled his fingers, his voice taking on the calm tone of a lecturer. "It began innocently enough. A few late nights at the casino. A thrill, nothing more. Asher had talent…. a good eye for the cards, a willingness to walk away when the table turned. But success is its own poison. He won early, and he believed that made him different. Special."

He glanced toward the skyline, as if seeing something beyond the glass. "The first loan was modest. He paid it back within twenty-four hours. The second, a bit more. Again, it cleared promptly. The third loan took longer, but he managed to pay it off. Each time, his confidence grew. Each time, he convinced himself he was untouchable."

Rivers' mouth curved faintly. "But no man is untouchable, Detective. Not even Asher Forest. The fourth loan was his undoing. He lost big. I told him once that the table has no memory. It doesn't care who you are, what you've built, how many millions you've made. It takes from anyone. That's the lesson he hadn't yet learned."

Kramer oversaw him. "And what would you have done, had he come to you to settle?"

"Worked with him," Rivers said, his tone firm but unbothered. "Shifted terms. Accepted equity. Negotiated an interest in his software company, perhaps. Men like Asher are rare. You don't break rare men. You keep them close."

Kramer leaned forward. "Some would say four and a half million reasons exist to put a man in a hospital bed."

Rivers didn't flinch. He folded his arms and met Kramer's gaze. "Detective, I'm not a thug in an alley. I'm a businessman. Violence is for amateurs. If Asher owed me, I had every reason to keep him alive, not beaten. Dead men don't pay debts. They don't innovate. They don't produce."

He let the words hang in the air, then added with quiet emphasis, "If someone wanted Asher silenced, it wasn't me."

Kramer studied him. Rivers' tone was steady, his eyes unwavering. Everything about him projected confidence, reason, and control. But the detective had been in this business too long to be fooled by polish. The tiny flicker of shock at Asher's name earlier told him enough: Rivers knew more than he admitted. Rivers rose smoothly, signaling the conversation was at its end. "Detective, I hope you find who did this. Asher is young, brilliant. A mind like his doesn't come along often. It would be a shame for the city to lose him."

He extended his hand once more, his grip steady, his smile just as warm as it had been at the start.

Kramer shook it but didn't return the smile. "We'll be in touch, Mr. Rivers."

As he left the office, Kramer caught sight of employees in glass cubicles, analysts tapping at keyboards, assistants juggling calls, and a receptionist smiling at a client. But to Kramer, the mask had already slipped for just a moment. And sometimes, a moment was all it took. To them, Grayson Rivers was still the gentleman in the fine suit, the businessman with the city at his fingertips.

Rivers stood by the window for a long moment, watching the detective's car pull away down the street. His reflection stared back at him in the glass…. smooth, composed, untouchable.

When the car disappeared, his smile slipped.

He turned back to his desk, picked up the phone, and dialed a private line. After two rings, a gruff voice answered.

"Yeah?"

Rivers' tone was cold now, stripped of charm. "Charles. Put Ray on, too."

A rustle, then another voice chimed in. "We're here, boss."

"You two assured me Asher Forest was handled." His voice sharpened, the temperature dropping with each syllable. "Imagine my surprise when a detective walked into my office this morning, asking questions. Imagine my shock when he told me Forest is alive."

A silence. Then Charles tried to cover. "We left him bad, really bad. Thought he was gone."

"You thought wrong," Rivers snapped. "And now you've made me look like a fool. If he wakes up, if he breathes one word to the wrong person, you'll answer to me. You understand?"

"Yes, boss," Charles muttered quickly.

Ray, less careful, chuckled nervously. "What do you want us to do, boss? Finish it, immediately?"

Rivers' voice dropped to a deadly calm. "Take care of him. Quietly. He's in the hospital, and you'd better pray to God he doesn't open his eyes. Because if he does, the two of you won't have time to regret it."

The line went silent.

Rivers set the phone down gently, his expression smooth again by the time his secretary knocked on the door to remind him of his noon meeting.

"Send them in," he said, voice warm, polished, as though nothing had happened at all.

Chapter 13: The Silent Witness

Detective Daniel Kramar returned to the hospital early that afternoon, his shoes clicking steadily across the linoleum. He expected to find Keith Forest and his daughter keeping vigil at the bedside, but the room was empty, only the faint hum of machines and the pale stillness of the man beneath them. The sight made him pause in the doorway. He had seen hundreds of victims sprawled across crime scenes, dozens more strung to hospital monitors after the violence of the streets found them. But something about Asher Forest felt different.

Maybe it was the contradiction. The family painted him as a flawless son… hardworking, brilliant, devoted. Yet the evidence Kramer had gathered told another story: a man drunk behind the wheel, a businessman cutting corners, a gambler in debt to one of the city's most dangerous men.

Kramer closed the door behind him and walked closer. The machines blinked rhythmically, their beeping steady, the oxygen hissing softly. Asher's face was swollen but recognizable, the bruises painting him a darker version of himself. His chest rose and fell, each breath a reminder that the line between life and death was thinner than anyone wanted to admit.

The detective pulled a chair close and sat down, leaning forward with his elbows on his knees. For a long while, he just stared, studying the man who had become the nexus of lies, debts, and violence.

"Tell me something, kid," Kramer murmured. His voice was low, private, like a confession. "Who did this to you? Who'd want to see you laid up like this? Because if you don't tell me, I've got to piece it together blind."

He rubbed a hand over his jaw, eyes narrowing. "I've got your family saying you were perfect. I've got Rivers saying you were reckless. I've got numbers that don't lie. But I don't have the name of the man who left you bleeding by that pond."

He sat back, sighing. "Help me out here. Give me something."

The silence mocked him. Just the monitors, ticking like a metronome, indifferent.

Kramer stayed that way for forty-five minutes, staring at Asher as if sheer might pull an answer out of him. The boy's eyelids twitched once, but it was nothing, just a reflex.

Then the door opened.

A nurse walked in, her steps too measured, her smile too brief. She wore the standard scrubs, a stethoscope draped around her neck. To anyone else, she might have looked like any other shift nurse making rounds.

But Kramer noticed things other people didn't.

Her eyes darted once toward him, lingering too long before settling on the clipboard at the foot of the bed. Her hands trembled faintly as she reached for the machines, adjusting them with motions that were just slightly off rhythm.

She cleared her throat. "What's your relationship to the patient?"

Kramer didn't move. "No relation. Detective. Local PD."

The words hung in the air.

The nurse froze, the blood draining from her face. She forced a nod, her voice tight. "I see." She fumbled with the blood pressure cuff, wrapping it around Asher's arm too quickly, then nearly dropping the thermometer as she placed it under his tongue.

Kramer leaned back in his chair, his eyes cool, saying nothing. He watched her body language: the stiff shoulders, the shallow breathing, the way she avoided his gaze.

She scribbled a number onto the chart with hurried strokes, then gathered her things. "Vitals look fine," she muttered and left the room.

The door clicked shut.

Kramer stayed still for a moment, his instincts prickling. Something wasn't right.

He stood, stepping into the hallway, and walked to the nurses' station. The head nurse looked up, recognizing him from the day before.

"Detective," she said. "Everything okay?"

"I need some information," Kramer said flatly. "Who was the nurse just in Mr. Forest's room? Mid-twenties, dark hair, blue scrubs, badge read 'Baker.'"

The head nurse frowned, flipping through her charts. "We don't have a Baker on staff today. Not in the ICU, not on this floor."

Kramer's stomach tightened. "You sure?"

"Positive. I know every nurse on the shift. No Baker here."

Kramer nodded slowly, his jaw working. As the woman turned back to her paperwork, he remembered something: a flash of ink on the nurse's forearm when she adjusted the cuff… a tattoo. Jagged lines formed a shape he recognized instantly.

The mark of the 27th Street Gang.

Kramer's pulse quickened, though his face betrayed nothing. Someone's reach had already slipped into the hospital.

He pulled out his phone and dialed the precinct. "This is Detective Kramer. I need a patrol car assigned immediately to the St. Central East General Hospital, specifically to the ICU wing. Protective detail for patient Asher Forest."

"What's the threat level?" the dispatcher asked.

"High," Kramer said curtly. "Suspicious individual posed as a nurse, left the room before I could stop her. Tattoo matches known associates of the 27th Street Gang. I want eyes on this room twenty-four/seven until further notice."

"Understood. Car will be dispatched."

Kramer hung up, his eyes narrowing as he turned back toward the ICU. The person who sent this nurse had failed this time. But the message was clear. They weren't finished with Asher.

As he pocketed his phone, the elevator doors opened. Keith and Carolina stepped out, each with leftover lunches in hand. Their faces were drawn, their eyes rimmed red, proof they'd been somewhere else, breaking apart.

They spotted Kramer immediately. Keith frowned. "Detective? You're here early this afternoon."

"Needed to check in," Kramer said evenly. He forced his voice to be steady, not ready to tell them how close their son had come to being silenced forever.

They walked back into Asher's room together. Kramer shut the door behind them.

Carolina sat down by her brother's bedside, her hand brushing his. She looked at Kramer, her voice hushed but urgent. "Do you know more? About these companies?"

Kramar folded his arms and leaned against the wall. "I met with some leads today. I can't go into details; it's still an active case. What I can tell you is that we're working every angle and every tip that comes in. Nothing's being ignored." Keith let out a low whistle, shaking his head in disbelief. "I can't… I can't even picture that number. I'm still replaying it in my head from earlier this morning."

Kramer studied them both. He expected more anger, denial, something. But what he saw was exhaustion, the kind that comes when grief and betrayal start to blur together.

"What else?" Keith pressed.

Kramer hesitated. His instincts screamed to mention the nurse, the tattoo, the shadow of the 27th Street Gang. But without proof, it would only terrify them. He swallowed it down.

"For now," he said carefully, "that's what I can share. There are still pieces missing, and not everyone's being candid with me. But I'll keep pressing. I'll get the answers."

Carolina looked back at her brother, tears slipping silently down her face. "What did you do, Asher?" she whispered. Kramar turned his gaze to the still figure on the bed, his thoughts hardening. You'd better wake up, kid, he thought grimly. Because if you don't, the only story left will be the one written by the men who put you here.

Outside the room, down the hall where no one was watching, the elevator dinged again. A janitor stepped off, pushing a cart piled with supplies. His uniform looked right, his ID badge clipped neatly, but if anyone had looked closely enough, they would have noticed his eyes scanning the hallway with too much intent, lingering too long on the door to Asher Forest's room.

But no one noticed.

Not yet. The room was quiet again once Kramer had left. Keith stood by the window, staring down at the street below. That's when he noticed the black-and-white patrol car pulling to the curb, its lights dark but its presence impossible to miss. The uniformed officer stepped out, leaning casually against the hood, scanning the front entrance with practiced eyes.

Keith's stomach turned. He motioned for Carolina to join him.

"Look," he whispered, nodding toward the car.

She pressed against the glass beside him, her coffee forgotten in her hand. For a long moment, they just stood there, watching the silent sentinel outside.

Carolina's throat tightened. "Why would they…?"

Keith shook his head, the words failing him. They looked at each other, unease flickering between them like static.

Then, slowly, their eyes shifted back to the bed, to Asher, pale and motionless, caught between life and death.

Neither spoke of the fear pressing against their hearts.

Something more was going on. Something bigger than drinking or debts. Something that might swallow all of them whole.

The patrol car lingered below, a quiet reminder that danger had already found its way inside. Keith and Carolina pressed their hands against the glass, silent, their faces pale in the city's afternoon glow.

They turned back to Asher, her brother, his son, still lying motionless beneath the hospital lights.

He gave no sign of hearing them. No movement, no words. But deep inside, Asher's mind was far from silent.

Chapter 14: The Debt Denied

Inside his mind, the hospital walls dissolved. The sterile lights, the quiet machines, and the smell of antiseptic all gave way to the warm haze of casino lights, the clatter of chips, and the soft shuffle of cards.

Asher was back at the table.

The green felt glowed under the overhead lamps. His hands moved confidently, brushing chips forward, stacking them, sliding them into place. Around him, the air buzzed with laughter, groans, the electric hum of risk and reward. His blood sang with it, a rhythm he couldn't quiet.

He had been here so many nights now that the casino felt more like home than the house he lived in.

The first loan had been easy, a hundred grand from Grayson Rivers, slipped into his account with nothing more than a handshake and a smile. He had paid it back within twenty-four hours. The second came just as smoothly; the stakes had doubled, and the repayment was swift. The third tested him, but still, he cleared it.

Every win fed him, every payout with interest swelled his chest. He wasn't just beating the game; he was bending the house and outwitting the man who staked him. For a moment, he believed he'd outgrown them all. The fourth loan loomed heavier…. $4.5 million. It slipped through his fingers like water he had sworn he could hold.

The dealer's voice lingered, unhurried, almost merciful. "Bust."

Chips vanished in a single sweep, the table devouring what had once felt unshakable.

Pressure knotted in his chest, a grinding ache that spread with each disappearing coin of his fortune.

Yet even then…gutted, hollowed, he clung to the lie that all losses were only temporary.

He saw himself leaving the table, adjusting his suit jacket as though brushing off dust, his lips curling into a smirk. I'll outpace it. One more deal. One more contract. I'll cover it, like I always do.

He was untouchable.

In his drifting memory, he was back in his office now, the one he had designed himself, sleek glass walls and clean lines, the logo of his software company etched proudly on the frosted glass.

Grayson Rivers was there, sitting opposite him in one of the leather guest chairs. He looked every bit the businessman: tailored suit, polished shoes, calm confidence that filled the room.

"Asher," Rivers said, his voice low and measured, "you know why I'm here."

Asher leaned back in his chair, lacing his fingers behind his head. He forced a smile, the kind of grin that had closed deals and charmed investors. "Yeah, yeah. The debt. Four and a half. I know the number."

Rivers tilted his head slightly. "Then you also know it isn't the kind of number that waits patiently."

Asher shrugged. "I told you, I've got contracts in the pipeline: municipal software, a new system for data integration. A couple more weeks, and I'll have the cash to cover it. Easy."

Rivers didn't move, didn't blink. "A couple more weeks can be a long time."

"Relax," Asher said, leaning forward now, elbows on the desk. "I've paid you before. Three times, as fast as lightning. You know I'm good for it."

Rivers' smile was faint, unreadable. "Three times, yes. And that's why I gave you the fourth. But don't confuse my confidence with infinite patience."

There was a flicker of irritation in Asher's chest, but he brushed it aside, flashing another grin. "Patience? Grayson, you'll get your money. Hell, maybe I'll double it and make us both happy. I'm on the edge of something huge here."

Rivers leaned back, steepling his fingers. "That's what every man at the table thinks until the house reminds him who's in charge."

Asher's smirk faltered for a fraction of a second, but he caught it, covering with bravado. "I'm not every man at the table. I'm Asher Forest."

Rivers let the silence hang between them, his gaze sharp, weighing him. Then, finally, he rose. "Remember the number, Asher. Four point five. Don't forget it."

Asher waved a hand dismissively as Rivers moved toward the door. "It's just numbers. I bend numbers for a living."

But when the door closed, the grin slipped from his face, and he pressed his palms hard against the desk.

In the haze of his subconscious, the memories blurred together, nights at the casino bleeding into mornings in the office, contracts signed with one hand while dice rattled in the other.

He saw himself laughing with friends, bottles of champagne spraying across private tables, women clinging to his arm as though he was untouchable. He saw himself staggering out of back rooms with stacks of chips in his pockets one night, empty-handed the next.

Every win fed the lie. Every loss he explained away.

I'm building an empire. I can afford this.

It's just a loan. I'll pay it back.

I'm smarter than the house. Always will be.

But in the quiet corners of his mind, the truth gnawed at him.

The fourth loan wasn't shrinking. It was growing. Every day he didn't repay, the weight of it pressed heavier on his chest.

Still, he brushed it off. Foolish or arrogant. maybe both…. he clung to the illusion that he was in control.

One last memory surfaced in the drift… Rivers returning, this time not to his office but to a meeting in a café, public enough to keep things civil, quiet enough to press the point.

Rivers stirred his coffee slowly, his eyes never leaving Asher's face. "You're running out of time."

Asher sipped his espresso, forcing a grin. "Time's all I need. Big deal's about to close. I'll cover it, and you'll get more than you asked for."

Rivers smiled thinly. "You think I'm worried about the money."

"Aren't you?" Asher shot back.

Rivers set his spoon down with precision. "I'm worried about men who believe they're invincible. They tend to fall the hardest."

Asher leaned back, waving him off. "I'm not falling. Not now. Not ever. I've got this under control."

Rivers held his gaze, then stood. "Control is the greatest illusion of all."

And with that, he left, the sound of the café's door chime echoing in Asher's ears long after the man was gone.

In the hospital bed, Asher's chest rose and fell steadily, but inside his mind, he was still smiling, still brushing it off.

The debts were numbers. The risks were games. Rivers was just another investor, no more dangerous than a banker with a ledger.

I'll outpace it, he told himself again. One more deal. One more contract. One more win.

The lie was his lullaby.

And in the stillness of his subconscious, he clung to it, even as the shadows around him began to close in.

Chapter 15: The Return

The low hum of machines was steady in Asher's room, but Keith and Carolina's thoughts had been anything but. Ever since spotting the patrol car lingering below, neither of them could settle. They kept circling back to the window, as if the cruiser itself were watching them, waiting for answers they didn't have.

"Why would they put a cop outside?" Carolina whispered, arms crossed tightly against her chest.

Keith didn't answer right away. He stood with his hands braced on the windowsill, jaw clenched, the lines around his eyes deepening. "Whatever Kramer isn't telling us… It's big enough that they think Asher's in danger. That's all I know."

Carolina's eyes flicked toward her brother's bed. "In danger from what? From whom?"

The silence that followed was heavier than the air in the room.

The sound of hurried footsteps in the hallway broke it. Both turned as the door swung open.

Aunt Robin Meyer stepped inside. Her presence filled the room the way sunlight broke through storm clouds, warm, grounding, unmistakably steady. She was older now than the memory Carolina had clung to, but her face still carried the same shape as their late mother's, the same softness in the eyes that had comforted them fifteen years ago when grief first swallowed their home.

"Robin," Keith breathed, relief flooding his voice.

Carolina rushed forward, wrapping her arms around her aunt. For a moment, she allowed herself to collapse into the hug, tears slipping down her cheeks. "You came," she whispered, clinging tightly.

"Of course I did," Robin said firmly, kissing the top of her niece's head. "I told you, nothing could keep me away. I caught the first flight I could."

When she pulled back, her eyes fell on Asher. Her breath hitched as she took in the sight of him: pale, bruised, motionless, tubes and wires tethering him to machines. She pressed a hand to her mouth, holding back a sob.

"Oh, my boy," she whispered, stepping closer. She reached out and brushed her hand over his hair the way she had when he was small. "What have you done to yourself?"

Her words weren't sharp, but they cut deep all the same.

Keith cleared his throat, stepping forward. "We… we don't know everything yet. The doctors are doing what they can. Kramer's still investigating."

Robin turned to him, her eyes sharp now despite the tears brimming. "Then tell me what you do know, Keith. Because from the sound of your voices on the phone, this isn't just some random attack. What's happening?"

Carolina's stomach twisted. She looked at her father, but Keith's gaze dropped.

Robin saw it. She always did. She stepped back, her voice quiet but unyielding. "You've been keeping things from me. Both of you."

Carolina's chest tightened. She wanted to hold it in, to carry the secret the way she had been for years, but something about her aunt's presence… the way she looked so much like her mother, broke the dam.

Her voice cracked as she spoke. "He… Asher… he wasn't perfect."

Keith turned sharply. "Carolina…."

But she went on, tears spilling now. "The first DUI. I bailed him out. He begged me not to tell anyone. Not you. Not dad. He swore it would never happen again, and I believed him. I thought I was protecting him, Aunt Robin. I thought I was helping."

The words fell into the room like stones dropped into water.

Robin didn't speak right away. She walked to the other chair and sat down, folding her hands in her lap. Her gaze stayed steady on Carolina, but her voice was softer now. "Protecting him by hiding the truth isn't protection at all. It's carrying his secrets for him. That's a heavyweight for a sister."

Carolina wiped her eyes, nodding miserably. "I see that now."

Robin turned her gaze to Keith. "And you? You had no idea?"

Keith's face was hard, but the shame beneath it was plain. "No. I didn't. And that's on me. I wanted to believe my son was flawless. I wanted to see the boy who built his first software in your basement, not the man who made reckless choices."

Robin studied him, then reached out, laying her hand over his. "You loved him so much you refused to see the cracks. That doesn't make you blind, Keith. It makes you a father. But now…" She looked back at Asher, her voice tightening. "Now those cracks are wide open, and you can't ignore them anymore."

The room fell silent again. The only sound was the monitor's steady beep.

Keith looked at his son, his voice breaking. "I just don't want to lose him, Robin. Not like I lost her."

Robin's own tears slipped free then, but her voice stayed firm. "Then fight for him. Stand in the truth, no matter how ugly it is. Because lies won't save him now." The room went silent. A soft knock came before the door opened, and a nurse stepped in, her scrubs whispering as she crossed to the monitors. The steady beeps filled the quiet while she checked the vitals. Robin leaned forward, her voice low. "How is he?"

The nurse glanced at the screen, then at Robin. "Stable for now," she said gently. "We're hoping for the best."

Robin's hands twisted in her lap, but she nodded. "Thank you."

The nurse offered a small, professional smile before making a note on her chart, and the room fell quiet again.

The room had grown heavy after Robin's sharp words about truth and lies. Even Carolina's breathing sounded uneven as she sat clutching her coffee cup. Keith hadn't moved from the chair by the window, his jaw set tight.

Finally, Robin broke the silence, her tone gentler now. "You've both been here since the beginning. Go home. Shower. Rest. You need your strength for what's ahead."

Keith shook his head immediately. "I'm not leaving him."

"Neither am I," Carolina said, her hand tightening around her brother's.

Robin stepped closer, her eyes firm but tender. "Yes, you are…both of you. You're no good to him, half-dead on your feet. I just got here… let me sit with him for a while. You'll be back before you know it."

Carolina looked at her father. "Dad…"

Keith exhaled slowly, the weight of exhaustion pressing on him. Dark circles pooled under his eyes, and his shoulders slumped. He hated to admit it, but Robin was right.

"I'll… I'll grab some clothes, come back in the morning," he said reluctantly. His voice cracked on the last word.

Carolina swallowed hard, brushing Asher's hair back once before standing. "I'll go too. We'll be back early, I promise."

Robin hugged them both at the door. "Get some sleep. I'll call if anything changes."

Keith hesitated a moment longer, looking back at his son. "Stay strong for him, Robin."

She nodded. "Always."

When they were gone, the room felt quieter, emptier. The hum of machines seemed louder without the shuffle of footsteps or the whisper of voices.

Robin sank into the chair at Asher's bedside, her eyes fixed on him. For a long time, she sat, her hand resting gently over his.

"You look just like her when you're lying there," she whispered finally, her throat thick. "Your mother. That same stubborn tilt of the jaw, even asleep. She fought to the very end. I see that same fight in you…. at least, I pray I do."

Her fingers trembled as she stroked his knuckles. "You always reminded me of her, Asher. That quick wit, that fire in your eyes when you wanted something. God, the way you'd storm into my kitchen when you were a teenager, talking about the next big idea, swearing you'd change the world with your computer."

Tears slipped down her cheeks as she let out a shaky laugh. "I believed you then. I still do. But somewhere along the way, you started believing your own lies more than the truth."

She leaned closer, her forehead almost touching his hand. "Your sister carried your secrets because she loved you. Your father blinded himself because he loved you. And me? I tried to stand in for your mother, but I wasn't her. I couldn't save you from yourself."

Her voice broke. "But I'm here now. And I'm begging you, don't make us lose you too."

The machines ticked on, indifferent.

Robin closed her eyes, pressing his hand against her cheek. "Wake up, Asher. Please. You've still got time to make this right. You've still got a chance to come back to us."

For a long while, she just sat that way, weeping softly, the sound muffled against his hand.

Finally, she straightened, wiping her tears with the back of her hand. She studied his face, pale and still, but in her heart she willed him to move, to give even the slightest sign.

"You've always been stubborn," she whispered. "Prove me right. Be stubborn now. Come back."

The monitor beeped steadily, unchanged.

Robin sat back in the chair, folding his hands inside both of hers. She kept her eyes on him, her vigil steady.

She would not look away. Not tonight.

Chapter 16: Lines in the Dark

Kramer's desk lamp carved a pale circle through the precinct's midnight. The rest of the bullpen was a scatter of screens sleeping, chairs shoved in by tired hands, a printer whirring to itself in the back like a restless animal. He'd been here long enough for the coffee to go cold twice. He pushed the third cup aside and leaned closer to the monitor.

Pause. Rewind. Play.

The hospital's north entrance- time-stamped 1:22 p.m. yesterday glided past in grainy color. Visitors flowed through the sliding glass doors, each captured and archived: a father with a stuffed bear, a delivery guy balancing brown bags, and a woman in blue scrubs, her hair tucked under a cap, a badge flashing past the camera's glare.

Kramer froze the frame and zoomed.

The badge name read Baker. Photo cropped just tight enough to hide the wrongness a stranger wouldn't see. He dragged the slider forward three seconds, her sleeve slipped as she adjusted the strap of her bag, exposing ink along the inner forearm: jagged black angles over three staggered bars. Most would think of it as art, but Kramer knew better.

Twenty-Seven.

He took a still, printed it, then pivoted to another screen and pulled up the gang unit's database. The 27th Street set had adapted well to the city's new cameras, long sleeves, hats low, temporary tattoos when it mattered. But some marks were pride, not costume. The triangles-with-bars motif had been theirs since the early 2000s, a stylized map of the avenues they claimed as their own.

He flipped to open cases. Recent intel flagged a woman who ran errands for the set, including pickups, drop-offs, and borrowing and returning uniforms. Real name: Lila Ortiz. Street name: Low Five. Five foot one. Three priors for fraud, one for assault with a weapon that didn't stick. An old intake photo stared back from the screen: wary eyes, an unwilling half-smile.

Kramer pulled the hospital footage again and ran it side by side with Ortiz's mug shot, noting the nose line match. Ear curve, match. The scar on the left brow you'd only see if you were looking for it there.

He made the call.

"Gang Intel."

"It's Kramer. I've got your Ortiz on a hospital camera from yesterday at the north entrance, wearing blue scrubs and a fake badge. Need everything you've got on her current affiliations and anyone she's been seen with in the last month."

The sergeant on the overnight sounded like gravel. "She's a runner for 27th. Keeps clean enough to work in daylight. Friend of a friend to the old guard, but lately we've heard she's doing freelance pickups for private work."

"Private like casino hosts? Or private like men who don't want their names in daylight?"

"Both. Any reason you're looking?"

"Someone impersonated a nurse in a high-profile victim's room," Kramer said, not offering more. "She shook when I said PD. Left fast. I want her pinned."

"We'll scrape cams on the blocks she usually runs. You want a BOLO?"

"Not yet," he said. "Quiet eyes first. If she's tied up with anyone bigger, I don't want them spooked."

He hung up and pulled up the hospital's internal logs. The head nurse had emailed a dump of badge swipes for the ICU wing, time, door, and ID. He sorted the list, scanning for Baker. Nothing. Whoever Ortiz was, she didn't come through doors that counted. He flipped to dock cameras and watched for an hour as carts, linen, trash, and uniforms blended in, wheels that could go anywhere without being watched too closely.

Uniform theft, or uniform loan? He sent a second email, this one to hospital security, short and blunt: initiate a code word protocol on Asher Forest's room; no one touches the patient without saying the word to the patrol officer outside. Change it daily.

He jotted it on a yellow sticky: "Code word: Demure." Random enough to be nonsense, specific enough to be remembered.

He stretched, vertebrae clicking, and stared at the map tacked on the corkboard beside his desk: the Great Pond where they'd found Asher, Rivers' tower in the financial district, the casino triangles, the hospital square. Pushpins connected by black thread, a childish craft turned into a quiet geometry of motive and means.

He traced the line from Rivers' office to the hospital with his finger

"Did you make that call?" he asked the air. "Or did someone under you try to impress the boss?"

There was a way these things went when the numbers got too big. First came the gentle reminders. Then the visit from a man with perfect cuffs and soft words about "alternatives." Then the not-so-gentle rumor. Only when men still didn't move did the violence show its face, and even then, if you were clever, you let someone else's hands throw the punch.

He saw Rivers' face in his memory: the momentary shock at being alive; the smooth return to sympathy; the glint that didn't quite make it to his pupils. The man wore a mask for a living. But masks slip when you think no one's looking.

He turned back to the hospital footage and fast-forwarded it. After Ortiz left Asher's room, she didn't head to the elevators or stairs. She slipped through a service corridor, pushed a door marked EMPLOYEES ONLY, and emerged fifteen minutes later at the loading dock behind a pallet of compressed oxygen tanks. A camera outside caught her exiting into the sunlight, her sleeve pushed down now, her head lowered, as the fake badge was tossed into a biohazard bin, where it would be incinerated by morning.

Clever. Not clever enough.

Kramer grabbed his coat. He sent a final note to the uniform sergeant: Rotate the patrol. Two officers, never alone. Post one at the door, one at the nurses' station. Check IDs and code word required.

Then he tugged off his tie and slung it over the chair. He closed his eyes for eight minutes with his boots on the edge of the desk, the precinct's hum drifting up around him like a tide. When the wall clock clicked 6:02, he opened them and stood. He gathered his notes, locked the folder under his arm, and headed out. The cruiser hummed as he steered into the gray wash of morning.

"Damn it," he muttered, gripping the wheel so hard his hands ached. "I know someone is behind this beating." He smacked the heel of his palm against the steering wheel once, sharp and hollow. "If those two business owners had just given me something…..anything…. we'd be closer to shutting this down."

His voice caught, frustration spilling into the empty car. He slammed the wheel again, harder this time, before dragging in a breath that rattled. For a few seconds, the anger and the helplessness sat heavy in his chest, threatening to overrun him.

Then he pressed it down, forcing his shoulders square. By the time the hospital came into view, the glass, catching the pale light of the face, was composed again. The family didn't need to see his cracks. They had enough of their own. The hospital lobby looked different when you knew it could bite, the same reception desk, the same volunteer's smile, the same floor polish in swirled crescents. But to Kramer, his eyes moved with intent; he scanned the room differently from those who kept their eyes low, noting which jackets sagged where the weight of a tool might sit; the janitor's cart with an extra shelf for nothing in particular.

He flashed his badge and rode the elevator up. The patrol officer at the ICU posted door had the posture of a man who used to run and still missed it…. late thirties, close haircut, jaw set. He clocked Kramer and straightened.

"Morning, Detective."

"You got the memo."

"Yes, sir. Code word, ID checks, no exceptions. We've turned away three scrubs who didn't have their story straight. Head nurse's not thrilled."

"She'll live," Kramer said. "What's the word?"

The officer's mouth quirked. "Demure."

"Good." He nodded at the second uniform down the hall. "Keep them paired. No one drifts."

He pushed the door open. Inside, the light was thin and blue from morning that hadn't entirely made up its mind yet. Aunt Robin had not moved far from the seat she'd claimed the night before. A blanket from somewhere in the hospital draped her knees, a paper cup cooling on the tray table, her hand wrapped around Asher's fingers as if she could anchor him by will.

She turned at the sound of the door and rose quickly, relief and steel in equal measure in her face. "Detective."

"You look like you didn't sleep," he said.

"I didn't." Her voice was hoarse, but steady. "Sit, please."

He took the chair Keith had been using, angled it so he could see both Robin and the door. Asher lay between them, a line neither crossed without permission. Kramer felt his jaw tighten at the thought; rooms like this made quiet promises, and men with power loved to step over quiet things. "I have a few updates," he began.

Robin's eyes fixed on him. "Are we safe here?"

Kramar weighed his answer, then gave her what he could. "Safer than yesterday. I've posted officers at the door and station. We've implemented a verification protocol. No one touches him without clearing it with my people."

The tiniest exhale left her, not relief so much as a breath she had forgotten to take. "Then something was wrong yesterday."

Kramar watched the heart monitor's green line rise and fall. He'd made a career out of not blinking first. "A person presented as a nurse and did not belong here. I confronted her. She left quickly. We're confirming her identity."

Robin's fingers tightened over Asher's hand. "And you didn't tell Keith and Carolina because…?"

"Because I'm still confirming facts," he said evenly. "And because panic helps no one. Once I can tell them everything and show them it's handled…. I will."

Her gaze sharpened. "And is it? Handled?"

"Contained," he said. "For the moment."

She studied him for a long beat, the lines at the corners of her eyes deepening with worry and a fight she'd fought too many times in too many rooms. "You remind me of a surgeon I met once," she said. "He wouldn't tell me how bad my sister's prognosis was because he couldn't stand the sound grief makes. He called it protecting me." She tipped her head. "Are you protecting us, Detective, or yourself?"

Kramer took it because she'd earned the right to throw it. "I'm protecting the case. And your nephew."

She nodded, accepting the boundary for now. "What do you need from me?"

"Eyes," he said. "You're the constant in this room until they get back. Staff rotation shifts every twelve. My uniforms rotate every eight. The danger arises when routine becomes comfortable. If anyone you don't recognize tries to touch him, you hit the call button and you shout the code. Don't be polite. Polite gets people buried."

Her chin lifted. "I wasn't raised polite," she said. "I was raised stubborn."

Something like a smile tugged at the corner of his mouth and vanished. He reached into his jacket and laid a small card on the tray: his number, written in block letters, followed by a second number below it. "Top one's me. The bottom is the front desk. If I don't pick up, the desk will ask you to state your name and the room number. They'll patch you straight through."

Robin touched the card on the small table and left it. "Thank you." He stood, turned the card over, and wrote his cell number on it, then turned it back. He could feel the edges of other conversations pressing at his jaw: the immaculate office where every smile felt rehearsed, the guys in the garage who moved boxes without asking what was inside, the casino host who'd long ago learned to keep his ledger in pencil.

"Robin," he said, and was surprised to hear himself use her name. "I'm going to say something that sounds cruel, and I don't mean it that way."

"Say it."

"You're the only one in this family who has looked directly at the truth since you walked in. Don't flinch now. If there is anything you remember, anything Asher said that sounded like bragging or worry, names, places, or a car that showed up too often, please tell me. And if you think of it tonight at two a.m., call me then."

She sat back, considering. "He came by my house two months ago without calling," she said slowly. "Pacing the kitchen like he was tracking satellites. He talked too fast, laughed too loud, and asked if I still had the lemon bars from the church bake sale in the freezer."

Kramer waited.

"He said something like… 'I've got a deadline like a tax man, Aunt Robin. But it's not the kind you can file an extension for.' I thought he meant a contract."

Kramer felt the phrase lock into place like a piece you'd been turning in your hand. He wrote the deadline like a tax man on his pad. "Did he say a name?"

"No." A pause. "He did glance out the window twice, like someone might be there. I told myself it was in my head. I tell myself lots of things to sleep at night."

"Which window?"

"Front. Street side."

He nodded. "Thank you."

They sat in the shared hush for a moment. From the hall came the low murmur of nurses trading notes, the squeak of rubber soles, the soft rasp of a cart's wheel that needed oil. The hospital was a place built to hold grief without comment.

Kramer's phone buzzed in his jacket. He checked the screen, turned slightly away to answer. "Kramer."

Gang intel again. "We scraped two blocks from Ortiz's usual runs," the sergeant said. "Caught her on a deli cam three hours after your time stamp. She meets a guy we know who goes by Croft. He runs low work for Rivers' accountant: cash drops, quiet pickups. We didn't have them together before, but now we do. You want us to pick either of them up?"

Kramer felt the click of the line from Rivers to Ortiz grow heavier in his mind. Croft. Accountant. Quiet pickups. Rivers would never call blood and ask for blood. He'd call a man who never got speeding tickets.

"Not yet," he said. "Stay on them. If they twitch toward this hospital, you put a hand on their shoulder."

He slid the phone away and met Robin's eyes. She'd watched his face like a nurse reads a monitor. "Bad news?" she asked.

"Useful news," he said. "Not for anyone else's ears yet."

She nodded. "You'll tell Keith and Carolina when…?"

"When telling helps more than it hurts," he said.

She didn't like it. He could see that. He didn't blame her.

He stood. "I'm going to do another pass of the lobby. Then I'll be down in the cafeteria for ten. I need caffeine and food. After that, I'll be back at the door."

"Detective," she said as he reached for the handle. He looked back. "Thank you for not pretending this is nothing."

"I don't have the talent for pretending," he said. "But I do have patience."

"Is that enough?"

"Sometimes," he said. "Sometimes you need timing too."

He stepped into the hall, pulled the door shut to the soft click that sealed the world on either side. He walked past the posted officer, caught his eye, and tapped two fingers to his own watch. The officer gave a fractional nod, attention sharpening.

In the cafeteria, Kramer bought coffee that tasted like it had been strained through a new filter, along with a plastic-wrapped banana muffin that was passed off as breakfast. He stood where he could see both the elevators and the front doors, letting the building move around him: security greeting a delivery, a woman arguing into a phone about insurance codes, a teenager in a school hoodie carrying flowers, his face a careful map of fear. The city flowed in and out of hospitals like tides of loss, hope, and inconvenience. Somewhere in that tide were the men who thought they owned current.

His phone buzzed again. Different tone. Unknown number.

"Kramar."

A soft male voice, educated. "Detective. You left your card with Mr. Rivers' receptionist a day or two ago. This is Evan Croft. I understand you're asking questions about a young man named Asher Forest."

Kramar's eyes narrowed, though his voice stayed pleasant. "I am."

"Mr. Rivers asked me to be helpful," Croft said. "The company prefers transparency."

"The company," Kramar echoed. "And your role in the company, Mr. Croft?"

"I assist with accounts," Croft replied smoothly. "Cash management. Liquidity events. The unglamorous work."

"I'm fond of unglamorous work," Kramar said. "Where would you like to meet to discuss it?"

"At the hospital," Croft said, his voice smooth as a glass conference table. "Perhaps the cafeteria. Ten minutes?"

Kramar glanced toward the ICU elevators, then back at the doors. The timing was no accident. How the hell did he know I was already here?

He didn't let it show. You didn't invite a cop onto your ground unless you wanted to measure what he knew and who else was nearby. He wants to see if Asher's room is being watched, Kramar thought. He played along.

"Ten minutes," Kramar said. "Buy your own coffee. The department's not in the business of subsidizing liquidity."

He hung up and stared at his reflection in the dark paneling across from him. For a second, he saw the outline of a man in a navy suit behind it, the city reflected in his cufflinks.

He took the stairs two at a time back to the ICU. "New protocol," he told the door officer. "If anyone without a badge asks about the patient in this room, you call me before you say a word."

"Yes, sir."

"Code word?"

"Demure."

"Right."

He cracked the door and leaned in. "Robin, I'll be downstairs for ten. If anyone comes who isn't in uniform and knows my name, you do not talk to them. If they say accountant or they say helpful, you push the button and you yell."

She stood with that stubborn line in her jaw. "Go," she said. "I'll be louder than you think."

"I don't doubt it."

He closed the door and headed back toward the elevator, coffee in one hand, the other already dialing the uniform at the lobby: Eyes up. A new player is coming, his name is Croft.

As he stepped into the elevator, the hospital announced a code blue on the second floor; life was dropping into crisis somewhere else. The doors slid shut, and his face ghosted in the brushed steel, already turning the angles of questions, as he'd lie to a man who claimed to love transparency.

Outside, the patrol car idled under a sky learning how to be day. Inside, a woman who had raised two children who weren't hers sat and held a man's hand as if she could keep him here by force of will.

Kramer rode down into the lobby. Kramar didn't wait in the cafeteria. He stayed near the main entrance, watching through the glass doors as Evan Croft's sleek frame appeared on the steps. When Croft spotted him,

Kramar gave a curt nod and gestured him inside to the lobby.

Almost immediately, Croft began. "So, Detective, how is young Mr. Forest? Which room is he in?" His tone was casual, but his eyes scanned the directory on the wall as though he might catch the name himself.

Kramar didn't blink. "Patient information is confidential," he said evenly.

Croft smiled thinly. "Of course, of course. I only meant…"

"I know what you meant." Kramar cut him off. His patience thinned with every sidelong glance and too-smooth shrug Croft gave. The man's body language said more than his words, nervous hands adjusting his cuff, eyes flicking toward the elevators, weight shifting like he wanted to be anywhere else.

Kramar leaned in just enough. "Tell me, Mr. Croft, any connection with the runners from the Twenty-Seventh Street gang?"

Croft's denial came quick, too quick. "Absolutely not."

But the twitch at his jaw and the way his gaze dropped to the floor betrayed something else.

Eight minutes later, Kramar had had enough. "If you don't have anything useful to contribute to this case, then this conversation's over." He turned, leading Croft back toward the doors, every step measured.

Croft lingered a moment under the fluorescent lights, that polished smile tugging at his lips, but he didn't argue. Kramar held the door for him and watched him leave, the knot in his gut tightening rather than easing. The second he stepped back inside, his phone buzzed. A plainclothes officer from the surveillance team was on the line.

"Detective, we've got eyes on Ortiz. She just slipped in through the loading dock, headed for the service elevator."

Kramar's pulse kicked. Croft's little diversion had just backfired.

Down in the bowels of the hospital, Ortiz moved quickly, her hood pulled up, hugging the wall as delivery trucks rattled and doors banged. She blended into the churn of orderlies and couriers wheeling carts, but the surveillance unit stayed two steps behind, carefully not to spook her.

The service elevator groaned as it carried her up. She stepped off on the main floor, scanning the hallway. The plainclothes officer trailing her gave a quiet signal. Within seconds, two more officers shifted into position, closing the distance without breaking stride.

Ortiz picked up her pace, weaving through the corridor. She passed a nurse's station, ignored the curious glance, and zeroed in on Asher's wing. Every step she took, she thought she was closer to finishing what she'd started.

Outside Asher's room, a uniformed officer snapped to attention as Kramar approached.

"Get Aunt Robin out of there," Kramar ordered. His voice was low but urgent. "Now. Walk her to the nurses' station."

The officer nodded, slipped inside, and within moments Aunt Robin emerged, her purse clutched tight against her chest. She didn't ask questions. One look at Kramar's face and she knew something wasn't right. Without hesitation, she allowed herself to be guided down the hall.

Only then did Kramar lift the radio.

"Hold your distance. Don't rush her. Let's see where she goes." Kramar stood out of sight.

Ortiz reached Asher's door. She hesitated only a second, then pushed it open. The room looked dim and quiet; the figure in the bed was still. She stepped inside and froze.

Two uniforms stepped from the shadows, blocking her exit. Kramar came into the room, and his voice dropped like a hammer.

"Game's over, Ortiz."

Her eyes darted for an exit, but the hall behind her had filled with blue. A hand seized her arm, twisted it back, the cold snap of cuffs locking tight.

Ortiz spat a curse, but Kramar just stared. Ortiz stiffened between the two uniforms, trying to resist. Kramar didn't waste time. He signaled toward the elevators.

"Get her out of here."

The group moved fast, keeping heads down through the main floor traffic. Outside, the evening air was thick and cool. The patrol car waited at the curb, engine running. Ortiz cursed under her breath as Kramar opened the rear door himself and guided her in with a firm hand.

The ride back to the precinct was quiet except for the occasional squawk of the radio. Ortiz stared straight ahead, jaw set, every muscle tight. Kramar didn't bother with small talk. He was already piecing together the threads of Croft's diversion, Ortiz's timing, and Asher's vulnerability. Too much lined up for coincidence.

At the station, procedure took over. The desk sergeant logged her in. Fingerprints were taken, jewelry and personal items sealed in a clear plastic bag. Her photo flashed once, twice under the harsh light of the booking camera.

Finally, she was led down a narrow hallway into an interview room with four walls, a bolted-down table, two chairs, and a clock that ticked louder than it should.

Kramar stepped in, dropped a slim folder onto the table, and took the seat across from her. He let the silence stretch. Ortiz shifted, the cuffs rattling against the metal armrest.

Only then did Kramar lean forward, voice low but sharp.

"Let's talk about why you were at that hospital."

Chapter 17: Pressure Points

The interview room smelled faintly of coffee and dust. Ortiz leaned back in the chair, arms crossed as far as the cuffs allowed. Her eyes followed Kramar as he opened the folder and let it sit on the table.

"You want to tell me why you were creeping around a hospital room?" Kramar asked, voice flat.

Ortiz shrugged. "I wasn't creeping. I heard Asher was laid up. I know him from the casino. Just wanted to check on a friend."

Kramar studied her without blinking. "Funny way to visit a friend. Through the service dock. Wearing a hood."

She shifted, the cuffs clinking against metal. "Didn't want to make a scene. Hospitals make me nervous."

Kramar flipped the papers one by one and came to a photo slid into view of Ortiz, younger, arms inked. He tapped the tattoo.

"Tell me about this."

Her jaw tightened. "It's nothing. I'm not in a gang."

"Right," Kramar said, leaning back. "Just some art. Nothing to do with the 27th Street boys."

"I said I'm not in a gang."

Kramar let the silence hang until it pressed the air out of the room. Then he leaned forward.

"What about Croft? What's he to you?"

Ortiz's eyes flickered. Too quick. "Don't know him like that."

Kramar slid another sheet across the table, her arrest record. "You were picked up running packages for him two years ago. Charges dropped. Does that ring a bell?"

She exhaled, long and slow. "I'm not his girl, alright? I work with other people."

"Names."

She hesitated, then muttered, "Ray and Charles."

Kramar narrowed his eyes. "Ray and Charles, who?"

"Just Ray and Charles. That's all I know them as. They're middle guys. I take what they pass, I don't ask questions."

Kramar scribbled the names down. "And who do Ray and Charles get their orders from?"

Her gaze dropped to the table. "Croft."

"And Croft gets them from…..?"

She shook her head. "I don't know. Whoever it is, they're out of my league. Way over."

Kramar tapped the folder again, voice sharpening. "You want to take the fall for this? Because I've got enough here to bury you. Attempted murder, gang affiliation, obstruction. You'll ride every charge. Or….." He leaned in, eyes hard. "You give me the chain. Start climbing up it."

Ortiz swallowed, her bravado cracking. "I'm not taking all the blame. Croft gave the order. That's what I know. That's it."

Kramar sat back, satisfied for now. He had names, a trail. And the feeling went deeper than even Ortiz realized. Kramar let the silence linger after Ortiz's last words, watching her chew her lip, eyes darting toward the clock. He'd gotten what he needed for now. Pushing harder might spook her back into refusing to talk.

He rose slowly, gathered the folder, and rapped twice on the door. An officer stepped in.

"Take her to holding," Kramar ordered. "Lock her down until arraignment."

Ortiz stiffened as the cuffs were re-secured. She threw one last glare over her shoulder as she was led out, but it landed flat.

Kramar waited until the door closed, then pulled his phone. He dialed the gang unit.

"Yeah, it's Kramar. I need intel on two names…. Ray and Charles. Could be runners, could be shot callers. Connected to Croft. See what you've got."

He dropped into the chair, pen tapping the folder. Ortiz had cracked, but only enough to confirm what he already suspected: Croft wasn't the top of the ladder. And whoever stood above him was pulling strings too heavy for Ortiz even to name. Kramar was still at his desk, scribbling notes, when the knock came. Twenty minutes later, Detective Harper from the gang unit stepped in, a folder tucked under her arm. She slid it across the desk.

"Ray and Charles," Harper said. "Been on our radar, but not enough to pull them in yet. Street-level operators, but smart. They know how to cover their tracks."

Kramar flipped the folder open. There were mug shots, arrest records, and surveillance notes.

"Ray Gutierrez," Harper continued. "Thirty-two. Petty charges back in the day. He boosted cars, small-time hustles. Worked his way up running dope for the 27th Street gang. He's graduated to being a 'runner' who delivers orders, collects cash, and ferries messages. Doesn't make decisions, moves the pieces."

Kramar scanned the page. "And Charles?"

"Charles Boone. Thirty-eight. A little heavier in the game. Known associate of Croft. He's careful, doesn't carry, and doesn't drive dirty. He has a small crew he uses for muscle, mostly kids trying to earn their stripes. Word is, he and Ray run together, Ray handles the legwork, Charles keeps the books, and makes sure Croft's orders get carried out."

Kramar leaned back in his chair. "So, they're conduits."

"Exactly," Harper said. "They're the bridge between Croft and the street hitters. And if Ortiz is tied in with them, it means she wasn't freelancing at that hospital. Somebody higher up gave the green light."

Kramar tapped the folder. "Croft."

Harper shook her head. "Maybe. But Croft doesn't usually get his hands dirty either. If he passed the order down, it's because somebody above him wanted it done."

Kramar closed the folder, the weight of it loud in the silence. "Then I need to know who that is." Harper flipped through her notes, then leaned forward.

"Narcotics have had eyes on Ray and Charles for a while now. They're tied into a pipeline running heavy dope through the east side. Nothing solid enough for an indictment yet, but I heard they're prepping to move in on a bust within the week."

"Can you give me an update within twenty-four hours after you speak with the unit?"

"Yes."

Kramar's pulse quickened. "So, if they go down…"

"You'll have your window," Harper cut in. "We don't want to spook them, so I'll keep your case quiet. I'll flag Narcotics, let them know we've got a parallel angle. If we can grab Ray and Charles at the bust, you'll get first crack at questioning them at the Twenty-Third Precinct. Clean, controlled, no surprises."

For the first time in days, Kramar felt a jolt of momentum. He stood, shaking Harper's hand firmly. "Appreciate it. Glad we're on the same page."

Harper nodded. "Just know this doesn't stop with Ray and Charles, with the amount of weight coming out of the east side. It is handled by someone high on the food chain, Someone you don't see yet."

Kramar watched her go, the folder still heavy in his hand. This was it, the break he'd been waiting for. If Ortiz was the spark, Ray and Charles were the fuse. And whoever stood at the other end of that line… that was the fire.

Back at the hospital, Aunt Robin sat once again at Asher's bedside. The soft beeping of the monitors filled the silence, but her nerves hummed louder. She had seen the officers outside his door exchanging code words, radios crackling, the sudden rush earlier in the day when Ortiz had been taken away in handcuffs. None of them had explained much, but they didn't have to. She could feel it in her bones—Asher was in deeper trouble than she could comprehend, and danger still circled.

Her hand trembled as she smoothed the blanket across his chest. "What did you get yourself into, baby?" she whispered, her voice breaking. Tears stung her eyes again.

Within the evening hour, the door opened softly. Keith and Carolina stepped in, their faces weary but expectant, hoping for even the slightest sign of change. They greeted her quietly, asking about Asher's condition, settling into the room with the heavy air of routine.

Robin forced a smile, drying her cheeks quickly before they could notice. She said nothing of the chaos that had unfolded just hours before. There was no reason to rattle them, no reason to add to the weight they already carried. She told herself she needed answers first from Kramar, from someone who could explain why her nephew's hospital room felt more like a crime scene than a place of healing.

So, she kept quiet. Let Keith and Carolina sit in peace beside Asher, unaware of the storm that had broken through his door.

Chapter 18: The High Place

As his family waited by his bedside. Asher lay still beneath the machines, his body unmoving. But deep inside the silence where monitors could not follow, his mind wandered…

Asher stood on a glass stage in his memory, the skyline at his back like a row of believers. He wore the suit he always chose for panels, the one that photographed as disciplined success rather than hungry excess. A conference banner arced behind him: Civic Data Summit. The moderator's question was still hanging in the air: What separates winners from everyone else?

"Clarity," Asher said, smiling into the bright. "And the willingness to act when others hesitate."

Polite laughter, pens scratching. He'd learned the cadence starts with the line that sounded like wisdom, then feeds them a story that confirms the myth they'd arrived with.

"In my first municipal pilot," he continued, "I was told to wait. Committees needed to be formed, subcommittees needed to be scheduled, and reports had to be written so that they could be written. I built the working model over a weekend and told them we'd go live if they liked the dashboard. We didn't ask permission to be useful."

More polite laughter. The moderator nodded. The audience leaned in, as if to code for "Teach me how to be you."

In the front row, he could see a young founder scribbling the word permission in a notebook, underlining it three times. Asher knew what he was doing to that kid. He did it anyway.

The memory shifted. Pride pulled a different slide to the surface.

He was in another conference room with a smaller company across the table, two men with tired eyes and decent products, the kind of founders who'd stayed up fixing bugs instead of practicing charm. Their prototype did one thing well. His platform did ten things adequately and one thing brilliantly: it promised a city that its chaos could be made legible.

"We'd love to partner," one of the men said, rubbing at a crease in his sleeve as if smoothing it would smooth the terms. "Your reach, our core module."

"Your core module is redundant in ours," Asher said, not unkindly. "But I admire the build quality." He slid the term sheet across the table. "Acquisition, not partnership. Cash and a six-month earnings if we choose to integrate. You'll be treated well."

The taller one swallowed. "That would end our company."

"It would save your product," Asher corrected, folding his hands. He'd learned this tone from men who'd acquired him in a simulation. "You want to stay alive or stay independent?"

They hesitated for the length of an old dream.

"We'll talk," the other said.

"You'll bring me their answer," Asher told his COO when the door closed. "And I want it by Friday."

"Hardball?" the COO asked, a shade of worry he thought Asher didn't notice.

"Mercy looks like hesitation on a balance sheet," Asher said.

He was right, and he knew it. That was the trouble.

The scene washed into another: Aunt Robin's kitchen, light slanting through the curtains, dust motes riding the beam like quiet planets. He'd come unannounced, carrying a pie he didn't eat and the impatience of a man who wanted praise without questions.

"You're working too hard," she said, reading his face like a familiar book.

"I'm building something," he said, opening the fridge and laughing when he found lemon bars wrapped in foil. "You still hoarding these?"

"You still pretending sugar calms nerves?" she asked.

He bit into one and winked. "Nerves are for people who don't know what they're doing."

"Or for people who know exactly," she said, placing a folded dish towel on the counter with ceremonial care. "Sit."

He sat because she could make him do things no board ever could.

"You scare me, Asher," she said. "Not because you're reckless with money. Because you're reckless with truth."

"I don't lie," he said reflexively.

"No?" She raised a brow. "What do you tell yourself you can't fail at?"

He grinned through the lemon curd. "Everything."

She smacked his hand with the towel, and he laughed like a boy. But later, alone in his car, he thought about her question and liked how the answer felt in his mouth. He repeated it at a red light, whispering it like a vow: Everything.

Pride picked up another scene like a card from a slick deck.

He was in the bullpen with his engineers, whiteboards snarled with arrows, a deadline pulsing red in the corner of the sprint board. An engineer named Sashi, thoughtful and careful, advocated for a rollback of a feature that looked appealing but struggled under usage spikes.

"It will fail at scale," she said. "The caching layer isn't…"

"The city demo is in 48 hours," Asher cut in. "We're not rolling back a headline feature because it might hiccup if a hundred thousand people click the same map tile at once."

"Because they will," Sashi said, not intimidated. "They always do."

"Then we patch during the demo," he said. "We'll preload data sets. Stagger the refresh calls. We'll make it look smooth, which buys us the time to make it smooth."

"That's deception," she said.

"That's theater," he answered. "We're in a business of actors who also build sets."

Sashi closed her eyes for a second, then nodded, because she was a professional. The demo went fine. The cache failed 72 hours later when the city embedded a traffic map on the homepage. They patched it in an hour. No one remembered. Asher did. He remembered that he'd chosen spectacle over caution and gotten away with it. Pride took that small win and fed it steroids.

He could feel the way pride had braided itself through the earlier sins, how it had poured drinks with a steady hand and told him he would walk a straight line; how it had sat in the casino's private room and whispered that numbers were obedient to men with will; how it had told him other people's companies were simply materials for his vision; how it had looked at Grayson Rivers, a man who ran currents under the city, and decided gravity would be kinder to him than to other men.

He let himself remember the first time he'd looked Rivers in the eye and decided he wasn't dangerous.

It had been at a charity gala. Rivers had worn a tux that fit like a threat you only noticed when you stepped on it. He had stood under a chandelier and spoken softly to a judge for a full minute without touching his elbow. Asher had watched the judge nod and laugh, and place a hand over his chest, as if agreement had weight.

Rivers turned and found Asher's gaze, then approached with the measured convenience of a man who never hurried.

"Mr. Forest," he'd said, as if the name itself were an asset he liked to inventory. "You build things that make chaos legible. I admire that."

"Chaos is a better salesman than order," Asher replied, pleased with himself.

Rivers had smiled, and it wasn't unkind. "Chaotic men make beautiful things," he said. "Until they mistake chaos for genius."

Asher had laughed, a little too loudly. He told himself later it was because he found the line clever. But pride knew a warning when it heard one and decided the appropriate response was to applaud.

The memory brightened, sharpened: his office again, the argument with Rivers that wasn't an argument because only one of them enjoyed friction. He heard his own voice… confident, clean… throwing numbers across the desk like they were dogs that would sit when told. Four point five had been a number, not a countdown. He had believed that completely.

"Just remember the number," Rivers had said at the door.

Asher had waved it away with a magician's flourish. Numbers behave.

The dark around the memory seemed to lean in.

"You were never humble," a voice in him said, not accusing, just locating the fact. His mother's voice? Aunt Robin's? His own, worn out and honest? He couldn't tell.

He called up other scenes to argue with it.

He stood in his father's garage on the night of the graduation party. He could smell charcoal, oil, the cheap sweetness of grocery-store cake. Keith had wrapped an arm around his shoulders in the doorway and said the thing fathers say when they have one perfect moment to place a stone in the road that won't be moved by weather: "I'm proud of you, son."

Asher had meant to say something softer than what came out. "I did it," he'd said, not we. He'd scanned the party for who would congratulate him next.

Later that night, on the phone with Carolina from the police station, he'd begged with sincerity but no humility. "Post it," he'd said. "Please, Lina. Don't tell Dad. I won't do it again." Pride had taught him the language of exceptions: Just this once because I am me.

When he drank again, he didn't call her. Pride hates witnesses more than it hates consequences.

Another flash: a competitor's CEO on a late-night panel, a man who'd bootstrapped slow and carefully. The moderator asked Asher to comment on the tenacity of small shops.

"They're artisans," Asher had said into the mic, smiling like he was framing a compliment. "But this city needs infrastructure, not art." The room laughed at the insult disguised as praise. He'd felt the adrenaline in it, the way it made him larger. On the sidewalk afterward, the other CEO walked past him without looking up. Asher watched him go and told himself the man's back was a moral for the losers. The moral was for him, and he missed it.

He remembered Carolina's face on a day he'd blown off lunch because he was "on a call." She'd waited an hour, eyes on the restaurant door like a wife in a movie; he'd texted Deal closing… rain check? With a confetti emoji because humility is allergic to punctuation that costs something.

She forgave him with a grace that made him reckless with grace.

The dark shifted again. Pride, having shown its montage, tried to close the curtain.
But another reel started on its own.

He was back at Aunt Robin's house, two months before the beating. He'd paced her kitchen, counting the lines of the tile because numbers soothe men who think they're losing control. He'd made a joke about taxes and deadlines, and she'd laughed softly, worried beneath it.

"Who are you looking for?" she'd asked when his eyes snapped to the window.

"No one," he'd said too fast. Then: "Everyone."

She'd poured him coffee he didn't drink and put lemon bars he didn't eat on a plate he pretended to appreciate. "You can't bring trouble to my door, Asher," she said evenly. "Do you think I don't see it?"

"I'm handling it," he said. He'd kissed her cheek and left, proud of himself for not trembling until he reached the sidewalk.

In the car, he had spoken out loud as if there were someone to audition for. "You're still you," he told the dashboard. "You don't bow."

He said it like a spell. Spells work until something larger than language refuses.

Pride wanted to be the villain of one scene and then leave. The truth was dumber: it was the temperature of the room he lived in. He had called his ruthlessness clarity, his appetite drive, and his dismissals efficiency. He had called his deafness to caution leadership. He had baptized his thirst as virtue and toasted it with borrowed money.

The table did not remember his name. The rooms did not love him. The men who lent him their currents admired him the way a craftsman admires a good blade: practical, until it cuts the wrong direction.

He tried, inside the dark, to imagine a sentence he could say now that would dislodge the reality his pride had constructed around him. The best he could manage was a small one.

I am not the exception.

The words unsettled him. He tried a different approach, one that had always soothed him. I am inevitable. It sounded childish suddenly, like a boy putting on his father's shoes.

He saw his father again, but not at the graduation party. He saw Keith at the kitchen table years earlier, bills in a stack, his hand rubbing his temple while Amelia coughed in the next room. Asher had been ten, standing in the doorway, watching a man be afraid and still fill out forms.

Keith had not called that fear clarity. Keith had not called to pay the mortgage genius. He had done the thing that kept the lights on. Pride, in the future, had mocked that simplicity as small. In the dark, Asher felt heat creep up his throat at the memory. I thought I had outgrown the need to survive, he realized. I thought surviving was beneath me.

He felt something loosen then, not a tube or a stitch, nothing useful to the room around his body. It was something in the logic that had carried him.

If I am not the exception, then I am a person, he thought, unsettled by the obviousness. If I am a person, I can break. If I can break, I must be careful.

The thought was so elementary, he wanted to laugh at it. The laugh didn't come. Another memory did.

The last time he'd seen Rivers in motion, not in an office, not at a gala, the previous time had been at the back of a club with lights so low the room felt uncommitted to being real. Rivers had sat with a man in a jacket that cost someone's month's rent, speaking to him like a teacher correcting a favorite student. The man had nodded, then nodded again, and then stopped nodding, listening intently. Rivers had placed a hand on the table between them, palm open, patient. Asher had thought, I'm that kind of value to him. He won't break me.

He understood, in the dark, that he had mistaken patience for mercy, valuation for affection. Pride had translated business into love. Rivers did not love anything he couldn't leverage.

The thought opened a door he had nailed shut from the inside. He looked, for the first time, toward the pond not at the water, not at the hands, not at the wooden echo of something breaking, but toward the moment before, when he'd decided to meet, when he'd decided he was still in control, when he'd decided they would talk like men who shared a city instead of men who were part of a market.

He tried to reach back and stop his own wrist from moving. The dark did not offer retakes.

Instead, it offered one more scene, not in glass, not in neon, not in charity halls. A hospital room in the small hours, a woman with his mother's face and his aunt's spine whispering to him like the old days when nightmares had shapes he could describe.

"You've always been stubborn," Aunt Robin said, somewhere near his skin. "Prove me right. Be stubborn now. Come back."

For the first time since he'd fallen into the quiet, pride didn't answer for him. Something smaller did. Something that had been pushed to the back when the crown got heavy. Pride had liked to say I. The smaller thing said we.

"We are in trouble," it said plainly. "We need help."

He didn't know if the word mattered beyond the border of his mind. He didn't know if Detective Kramer would ever hear him, if his father would ever forgive him, if his sister would ever look at him without the bruised bewilderment that had been on her face in every memory since.

He only knew the dark had finally allowed the sentence: I am not the exception.

A monitor somewhere kept time. The line rose, fell, and then rose again. He could not feel it. He could only count.

Outside the dark, the morning shifted gears into day. A chair scraped. Paper whispered. A uniform officer cleared his throat in the hall. A detective read and reread a transcript of a man named Croft declaring himself harmless. A woman with lemon bars in her freezer squeezed a young man's fingers as if she were arguing with an ocean.

Inside the dark, pride….at last…sat down.

He did not know if it would stand up again when the light came. He did not know if there would be light.

But something that had always needed to sit had finally found a chair.

And for the first time, the story did not move because he pushed it.

It moved because he let go.

Chapter 19: The Bust

The next morning, the monitor in Asher's hospital room kept its same fragile rhythm, rise, fall, rise. His aunt's hand never left his hand, whispering prayers as if each word could weigh down the drifting line and anchor it steadily. His father dozed in the chair by the window, head bowed, exhaustion settling heavier than grief.

Detective Kramer lingered outside the doorway long enough to feel the pull of their waiting. He wanted the same thing they did for Asher to wake up, too, but he knew that wanting it wouldn't stop Rivers. Justice demanded pressure, not patience. Suddenly, his phone rang; it was Harper. He quickly answered it.

"It's on," Harper said. "Narcotics has the greenlight. Warehouse on East Ninety-Fourth. We hit tomorrow, zero five hundred."

Kramar stood taller with a smile on his face. "Ray and Charles?"

"Both expected on-site. They'll be moving product. We'll sweep the place, but you'll have your window. Narcotics will run them through intake. Once they're cleared, they're yours at Twenty-Third. But Kramar…" Her voice sharpened. "This is going to be big. Don't spook the higher-ups until we know who we've really got."

Kramar scribbled the details, heart hammering. "Copy that."

He hung up, staring at the clock on the wall at the nurse's station, less than twenty-four hours. Tomorrow morning, everything could change. Kramar stepped quietly back into Asher's room. The steady hum of machines filled the silence, broken only by the soft creak of Aunt Robin rising from her chair. Keith and Carolina looked up at him expectantly, their faces drawn with worry.

"I wanted to update you," Kramar began, his tone measured. "We're pursuing leads. There may be two other individuals connected to what happened to Asher. I can't go into details, but we're moving on them soon."

Keith leaned forward, eyes sharp. "What are their names? Who do they work for? Are they connected to the casino?"

Kramar lifted a hand, polite but firm. "Those are valid questions, Keith, but I can't answer them right now. This is part of an ongoing investigation. Other specialized units are investigating additional criminal activity associated with these men. That's all I can say at the moment but know this: we are working the case."

Keith sat back, frustrated but silent.

Kramar shifted his weight, glancing toward Asher's still form. "I'll also continue to monitor his condition closely. And there will be officers stationed outside his room around the clock for protection."

Carolina's voice broke the pause. "Why does Asher need security?"

The room went still. Kramar's eyes swept over them, then he said, "It's for the best."

He turned toward the door, hand already on the knob. "If you think of anything…. anything at all…please don't hesitate to call me."

The door closed softly behind him, leaving the family in a silence heavier than before. Kramar lingered just outside Asher's door, the muffled hum of machines filtering through the walls. His jaw tightened. He hated holding back from the family watching their eyes search his face for answers he couldn't give.

He glanced at the uniformed officer posted outside. "Remember the protocol," he said, his voice clipped. The officer nodded firmly, settling into his watch.

Kramar turned down the hall, his shoes echoing softly against the linoleum. By the time he reached the elevator, his shoulders were tight with frustration. He pressed the button, exhaling through his teeth.

Once in his car, he sat for a moment, staring at the steering wheel. The day weighed heavy questions he couldn't answer, threats he couldn't yet stop. But under the frustration was a thin thread of relief. The narcotics unit was moving tomorrow. Ray and Charles would finally be in reach.

He gripped the wheel tighter, a spark of determination cutting through the fatigue. The interrogation was coming. And when it did, Kramar intended to peel back every layer until the whole rotten structure was exposed. Kramar started his car and pulled away from the hospital, the city lights sliding past his windshield. At the precinct, he sank into his chair, the case file spread wide across his desk. He retraced every lead, every loose thread, searching for the piece that would tie it all together.

But he knew the truth: Ray and Charles were the handles he needed. Once they were in custody, the picture would sharpen.

The hours dragged. He kept glancing at the clock, wishing the hands forward to five a.m. By eight that night, exhaustion finally drove him to call it a day. Before leaving, he thumbed a quick text to Harper: *See you at 23rd.*

Her reply came almost at once: *Absolutely.*

Kramar slipped the phone into his pocket. The day had been long, heavy, but he wasn't leaving with frustration this time. Tonight, he left the police station with something closer to hope instead of doubt.

He locked up the file, headed out to his car, and drove home through the quiet streets, already counting down the hours until dawn. By five a.m., Kramar was across town at the Twenty-Third Precinct, the staging ground for the morning's raid. The waiting was over. The long night of turning case files in his head had given way to action. The briefing room reeked of stale coffee and gun oil. Officers from Narcotics huddled around a wall map dotted with pushpins and scribbled notes. Detective Harper stood at the front, laser pointer in hand.

"Target's a warehouse off East Ninety-Fourth," she said. "Front's a used auto parts business, but intel says the real action's in the back, dope moving in bulk, cut and packaged. Our CI puts Ray Gutierrez and Charles Boone on-site this early morning, supervising a shipment."

Kramar sat in the back, silent but alert. Harper had kept her word; she'd tied his case into theirs without flagging his true interest. He was just another detective on the op paper. But in his mind, today was different. Today was his chance.

The operation moved fast. By dusk, unmarked vans were staged three blocks out, SWAT gearing up. Narcotics units slid silencers onto rifles, checked comms. Kramar adjusted his vest, his hands brushing the folder of Ortiz's statements tucked into his bag.

"On my go," Harper's voice crackled over the comms as the convoy rolled toward the warehouse.

The takedown hit like thunder. A battering ram splintered the side door while flash-bangs burst light across the dark alley. Shouts of "Police! Hands!" cut through the chaos. Shadows scrambled inside as the runners, lookouts, and panicked kids bolted for the exits.

Kramar followed the entry team in. The air was heavy with the reek of cut cocaine and diesel. Tables covered with scales and baggies stood abandoned mid-process.

"Clear right!"

"Suspect down!"

"Hands where I can see 'em!"

In the corner, Ray was caught trying to shove a duffel bag out the back window. He froze under the red dot of a rifle, dropping flat as two uniforms cuffed him.

Across the room, Charles Boone had his hands raised high, sweat running down his face. He didn't fight as SWAT pressed him to the ground.

Within minutes, the warehouse was locked down, and suspects were lined up along the wall. Narcotics were already logging evidence, bricks of product stacked like cinder blocks, cash bundles rubber-banded into evidence bags.

Harper pulled off her helmet and scanned the room. She caught Kramar's eye and gave the faintest nod. The message was clear: they were now yours.

Kramar's pulse hammered. Ray and Charles. Finally in cuffs. Finally, within reach. By the time Narcotics finished intake and moved them to the Twenty-Third, the real work could begin.

Chapter 20: The Interrogations

Charles Boone slouched in the metal chair, eyes fixed on the two-way mirror. He'd been in that room barely three hours, but it felt like half a lifetime. No phone, no clock, just the hum of fluorescent lights and the occasional scrape of his cuffs when he shifted. Across the hall, Ray Gutierrez wasn't doing much better. He'd run his mouth during intake, loud and defiant, but the silence of the interview room had eaten that bravado clean. Now he tapped his foot in nervous bursts, staring at the door like it owed him an answer. The first round of questioning had been enough for Kramar to know they were holding back. Croft's name was on the table, but the man pulling the strings wasn't. Until that name came out of one of their mouths, the case was scaffolding without a frame. Kramar dropped his coat on the back of the chair in the observation booth, cracked his knuckles once, and looked through the glass at Charles: big shoulders, gold tooth, arms crossed in practiced defiance. They'd rehearsed silence, he thought, but silence had a shelf life.

It was time for round two.

He stepped into Charles's room first. Charles looked up when Kramer came back into the room, the smirk already in place. He'd had an hour to rehearse and minutes to convince himself that silence was armor.

Kramer didn't bother with pleasantries. He set two files on the table with a deliberate thud; one was Ray's transcript from earlier, and the other was his. He didn't open either one. He just tapped them with a forefinger.

"Funny thing about stories," Kramer said. "When you tell them twice, the cracks show."

Charles leaned back, arms crossed, flashing that gold tooth like it was a badge of honor. "What cracks? I told you everything I got."

Kramer flipped the first file open and read a line in a monotone voice. "'I don't know the man in the hospital.' Now here's Ray's version: 'We were supposed to make sure the job was finished.'" He closed the file. "See the problem?"

Charles shifted, jaw tightening. "Ray talks too much."

"Ray talks just enough," Kramer said evenly. "Enough to tell me you weren't freelancing. Enough to tell me you got orders." He leaned forward, voice low. "And we both know you don't take orders from Croft. Croft's a middleman. You're not scared of Croft. You're scared of the man over him."

Charles's jaw flexed, but he kept his eyes steady. "You keep chasing ghosts, detective. Let me know when you catch one."

Kramer studied him a moment, then reached into the second file. He slid across a photo of Charles at the warehouse, phone pressed to his ear. Timestamp: the same day, Ortiz was in the hospital.

"Tell me again how you don't know what I'm talking about," Kramer said.

Charles's eyes flicked to the photo and back. "That's a phone call. Congratulations. People make those every day."

"Not people under surveillance for conspiracy," Kramer said. He let the silence stretch until it pressed against the walls. "Here's the thing, Charles. I don't need you to confess. I need you to keep lying. Because every time you do, I compare it to Ray's statement, and the ADA gets another reason to stack charges against you. You want forty years on paper? Or you want to be useful?"

Charles's smirk wavered. He leaned forward, elbows on the table, trying to claw back control. "You think I'm gonna give you a name? You don't know how this city works. You don't say his name. You don't even think about it if you want to breathe."

Kramer didn't blink. "Then don't say it. Spell it. Draw it. Whisper it. I don't care how. But we both know where this leads, and it's not Croft."

Charles stared at him, a muscle twitching in his jaw. For a long moment, the silence thickened. Then he leaned back again, covering the slip with a grin. "You'll get nothing from me. Ray's the weak one. Go squeeze him."

Kramer stood, gathering the files. "Oh, I intend to."

He left Charles in the room, the smirk gone the moment the door shut, replaced by the uneasy twitch of a man who'd just realized the walls were closer than he thought. In the other room, Ray sat slouched in the chair, arms limp at his sides, eyes fixed on the table. Kramer could see red lines etched across his eyes, the way his jaw worked as if he were chewing something sour.

Kramer came in without a file this time, just a single notepad and a pen. He dropped them gently on the table and sat across from him.

"You know what I like about two-man jobs?" Kramer asked, voice conversational.

Ray didn't answer.

"One of you always thinks he's the tough guy. The other one knows better." Kramer leaned back. "Today, Charles told me a story. Now you're going to tell me his mistakes."

Ray shook his head. "Charles doesn't make mistakes."

"Really?" Kramer said, raising his brows. "Because he just told me you talk too much."

Ray's eyes flicked up, startled. "He said that?"

Kramer let a small smile creep across his face. "Said you were the weak link. Said you'd fold first. Said you weren't built for the kind of heat coming your way." He let the words land. "That's loyalty, huh?"

Ray's fingers twitched against the tabletop. "He didn't mean that. He's just running his mouth."

"Maybe," Kramer said, leaning forward now, lowering his voice. "Or maybe he already gave me what I need, and I'm just waiting for you to prove him right."

Ray swallowed hard. His foot started tapping against the floor. "He doesn't know anything."

"Then we're in luck," Kramer said smoothly, sliding the pen toward him. "Because I only need one of you to tell me the truth."

Ray stared at the pen like it might bite him. "Look, man… I didn't sign up for this. We were supposed to make sure the job was finished. That's it."

Kramar leaned in, voice steady. "Finished? You and I both know jobs like this don't come out of thin air. Somebody gave the order." He let the silence hang, then added, "Ortiz already gave me your names. And Croft. But Croft?" He shook his head. "Croft doesn't run this show. So, who does?"

Ray's mouth opened, closed. Sweat beaded at his hairline. "You don't understand. If I say it…." He cut himself off, shaking his head violently.

Kramer leaned in, voice low and steady. "If you don't say it, you go down for all of it. Conspiracy. Attempted murder. You'll rot while the person who's in charge finds two more muscle boys and forgets your name. If you do say it, I can put you on a cooperation agreement. Less time. Maybe even a deal."

Ray's tapping foot went still. His voice dropped to a whisper. "It was him. Rivers."

Kramer didn't react, didn't smile. He just let the word settle between them like a weight. "Repeat it."

Ray's eyes darted to the mirror, to the camera, to the ceiling as though checking who might be listening. Then he said it louder, clearer: "It was Grayson Rivers. He gave the order."

Kramer clicked his pen once, jotting the name with deliberate strokes. "Good," he said softly. "Now we're getting somewhere."

Ray sagged in his chair, the relief of finally saying it fighting with the terror of what it meant. Kramer closed his notebook and stood. Ray didn't look at him; he was staring at the wall now, shoulders hunched, as if saying Rivers' name had taken the last of his strength.

In the hall, the uniform on duty raised a brow. "Anything?"

Kramer gave the slightest nod. "Enough."

He walked past Charles's room. The big man was still sitting tall, chin up, jaw set, the smirk stapled back in place like a badge of honor. He didn't know his partner had already folded. He didn't know the name was out.

Kramer kept moving, down the corridor, through the hum of the precinct. He didn't let himself smile, but he felt the edge of one inside his chest. After a week of shadows, he had a name written on paper, in ink.

Grayson Rivers.

He pulled out his phone and sent a short text to the ADA: *We have him. Preparing warrants.*

The reply came fast: *Get it clean. No mistakes.*

Kramar slipped the phone back into his pocket and paused by the precinct's narrow window. The city stretched beyond streets where men like Rivers built their empires on fear and silence. But silence had broken this afternoon.

By late afternoon, word filtered back through the hallways of Twenty-Third. Narcotics had moved on Croft. Ortiz's statement was enough to greenlight the warrant, and a tactical team picked him up outside a rented condo in the Heights: no theatrics, no chase, just a man caught flat-footed as the walls closed in.

Kramar read the brief report, his jaw tight. Croft was now in custody, boxed and bagged. But his eyes were already on the next rung of the ladder. Rivers. Croft was just a gatekeeper; the man who pulled the real strings still walked free.

He closed the file, pushed it aside, and reached for a fresh legal pad. Croft would be processed, but Rivers required precision. The margin for error was gone.

Tomorrow wasn't just about an arrest; it was about cutting the head off the snake.

Chapter 21: The Takedown

By morning, the city's gray had sharpened into steel. Kramer sat in the briefing room with a stack of files spread out like cards, including warrants in progress, subpoenas ready for signatures, and a line of phone records tracing Croft's number to Rivers' holding company.

On the whiteboard, four names were written in block letters: Ortiz. Gutierrez. Boone. Croft. A red line cut through all the names, and from there, a heavier line went to RIVERS.

"Follow the money," Kramer said, tapping the board with a marker. "That's where he always hides."

Two detectives leaned in, flipping through the bookkeeping reports that had been pulled overnight. Rivers' empire looked clean at first glance, with construction contracts, tech investments, and property management firms. But buried in the ledgers were knots: companies were swallowed, assets were absorbed, and owners vanished without fanfare.

"Here," Detective Velez said, circling a name. "Mont Printer Solutions. The CEO disappeared eighteen months ago. Business folded into a Rivers subsidiary six weeks later."

"Same with Allership Dynamics," another detective added. "The founder never resurfaced. Company absorbed."

Kramer nodded. "Pattern's consistent. Debt, disappearance, acquisition. He's been doing this for years."

The room was quiet for a moment, the weight of it sinking in.

Kramer capped the marker. "This isn't about one man in a hospital bed. Rivers built a machine that eats people and sells the bones as assets. Today, we shut it down."

The plan came together quickly: surveillance on Rivers' office, a tactical team staged two blocks away, and the financial crimes unit ready to seize records. Kramer would lead the arrest himself. He didn't trust anyone else to put the cuffs on.

By nine, the team was suited up… wearing plain clothes for cover, with tactical gear staged in vans. Kramer tucked the warrant into his jacket, its weight heavier than paper should be.

He checked his phone one last time. A message from Aunt Robin: Do you have any news?

He typed back, "Working on it." Tell him to hold on.

He slipped the phone away, jaw tight. "Let's go get him." Rivers' office was glass and walnut, perched high above the city, as if it had been built to remind everyone who ran it. Floor-to-ceiling windows bled daylight across a desk cleared to surgical precision…no papers, no clutter, just a single fountain pen laid horizontal across a leather blotter.

When Kramer entered with two detectives flanking, Rivers didn't rise. He didn't even look surprised. He closed the file he'd been reading, smoothed his cuffs, and leaned back in the chair.

"Detective," Rivers said, voice calm as polished stone. "What can I do for you today?"

Kramer laid the warrant on the desk, the paper stark against the dark leather. "Grayson Rivers, you're under arrest for conspiracy, fraud, and obstruction of justice. More charges will follow." Rivers' eyes flicked to the warrant, then back to Kramar. "Fraud?" He smiled faintly. "Detective, every contract in that file was signed willingly. Men come to me drowning. I offer them a lifeboat. If they can't swim, is that my crime?"

"Funny thing," Kramar said evenly. "Lifeboats don't usually end with men disappearing."

A flicker, the most minor crack crossed Rivers' face. It was gone in an instant. "You have no body. No witness."

"I have Charles. I have Ray. I have Croft. And I have a ledger full of ghosts," Kramar said. "That's enough to start."

Around them, officers were already in motion, seizing files and laptops.

Rivers rose finally, slow and deliberate, buttoning his jacket as if preparing for a meeting instead of an arrest. "You should be careful, Detective. Sometimes the man you think you've caught is only the shadow he leaves on the wall."

Kramer stepped forward, cuffs in hand. "Turn around."

For a moment, it seemed Rivers might resist. The air tightened, and every detective in the room tensed, hands drifting toward holsters. Then Rivers smiled again, soft and dangerous, and turned with measured ease.

The cuffs clicked around his wrists.

Kramer leaned in, his voice low, meant only for Rivers' ear. "Shadows don't last long in daylight."

Rivers tilted his head, still smiling. "Daylight fades, Detective. Remember that."

They walked him out through the lobby, suits and secretaries frozen mid-step as the man they'd followed for years was led past them in steel. Cameras from surveillance vans caught the moment. By the time Rivers was loaded into the back of the cruiser, the city already felt different, like a current had shifted.

Kramer stood on the curb, watching the door slam shut. For the first time in a week, the knot in his chest loosened.

The fight wasn't over until Asher Forest opened his eyes and spoke. But Rivers was in custody, and the company he'd built had finally jammed.

Chapter 22: The Silent Wall

The precinct had a different hum when a man like Rivers walked through it in cuffs. Not louder, but quieter. Detectives paused mid-sentence, eyes trailing him like gravity bent their attention. Uniforms stood straighter. Even the coffee machine seemed to hiss more softly, as if the building had just received power.

Rivers didn't look at the cuffs. He didn't have to. He wore them like they were ornamental, a pair of silver cufflinks that happened to click shut. When the transport officers guided him past the bullpen, he offered a faint nod, as though acknowledging their service. No defiance. No panic. Just calm.

Kramer watched from the hall outside Interview Room Four. The arrest warrant still weighed in his pocket, heavier now that it had delivered its prize. For a moment, he let himself feel the satisfaction of the city's untouchable man sitting on a bench, waiting. Then his phone buzzed.

Update from St. Central East's Hospital: Forest stable. No change.

Kramer exhaled, tucking the phone away. He needed the kid conscious. Paper trails and mid-level confessions-built scaffolds; testimony drove nails. Without Asher's words, Rivers could walk through the cracks.

The squad room buzzed as Velez dropped a stack of ledgers on Kramer's desk. "Financial Crimes had the paper trail from last night. Add in what we seized today, and it all matches," Velez said. "Two disappearances matched to acquisitions: Mont Printer Solutions and Allership Dynamics. Both founders vanished. Rivers swallowed the companies whole six weeks later."

Kramer scanned the files, jaw tightening. "That's two businessmen who didn't just lose their shirts, but they lost their lives." He tapped the folder shut. "Let's see if he's got an answer for that."

The room was designed for pressure, with a bare table, two chairs, and a camera in the corner. Rivers was already seated when Kramer stepped inside, posture loose, cuffed hands resting like he'd chosen the position himself. He smiled faintly, as though Kramer had been late to an appointment.

"Grayson Rivers," Kramar said, his voice smooth as polished glass. "I trust the drive over was comfortable?"

Kramer dropped the ledgers onto the table. "Let's talk about your books."

Rivers glanced at the files, then back at Kramer, unbothered. "You'll find them thorough. My accountants are meticulous."

"Thorough enough to hide two vanished men, Kramer said, flipping the first folder open. Mont Printer Solutions. Allership Dynamics. Both CEOs disappear. You acquired both companies within weeks." He slid photos across the table with smiling faces of men who'd been alive before they'd crossed Rivers. "What happened to them?"

Rivers studied the photos for a moment. His expression didn't change. "Business is a demanding current, Detective. Some men swim, others tire. I offered them lifeboats. If they chose to sink, that is not my crime."

Kramer leaned forward. "They didn't drown. They disappeared. You tell me it's a coincidence two men vanish right before you profit?"

Rivers steepled his hands. "Coincidence is the language of men who can't prove patterns."

Kramer's jaw flexed. He slid another sheet forward, revealing phone records tied to Croft, as well as meetings logged against his shell companies. "Croft calls your offices. Charles and Ray admit they were on your clock. Ortiz flips, says they cased the hospital under orders. That's your chain, Rivers. You."

Rivers' smile sharpened at the edges. "Charles and Ray are unreliable narrators. Croft, even less so, and I don't know an Ortiz. Desperation breeds stories. You should know this; you listen to them every day."

"Then tell me yours," Kramer said.

"I already have," Rivers replied. "I run businesses. I acquire. I expand. Some men resent success."

Hours bled out like water through a sieve. Kramer pressed patterns of fraud, unexplained wire transfers, and testimonies that painted Rivers as the architect. Rivers answered each calmly, never raising his voice, never asking for a lawyer. He smoothed every accusation into a philosophy, every document into an anecdote about risk and reward.

By the third hour, Kramer felt the weight behind his eyes, the ache in his jaw from clenching. Rivers sat opposite, serene, as though he'd been built for interrogation.

Finally, Kramer snapped the folder shut. "You're good, I'll give you that. But paper trails don't vanish. And when Forest wakes up, his testimony ties this all together."

For the first time, Rivers' brow lifted. Not alarmed but amused. "Ah, the boy." He leaned back. "A pity to hang your hopes on someone who can't speak."

Kramer stood, gathering the files, hiding the exhaustion in his shoulders. "He'll speak. And when he does, you'll finally run out of answers."

Rivers adjusted his cuffs, perfectly calm. "Detective, if I were guilty, don't you think I'd have asked for an attorney by now?"

Kramer left the room without replying, the door clicking shut like a verdict he didn't yet have the power to deliver.

In the hall, he leaned against the wall, rubbing his temples. Rivers was slick, untouchable in posture, a man who'd rehearsed this dance for years. No crack. No slip. Which meant Asher Forest wasn't just a victim anymore. He was the linchpin. Kramar pulled out his phone, staring at the hospital's number. "Hold on, kid," he muttered. "You're the one who brings him down." He sat back at his desk.

After a couple more hours of paperwork and reviewing financial records, Kramar's eyes began to blur the numbers together. Exhaustion set in. He finally pushed the files aside and called it a day. The streets were quiet by the time he left the precinct, more peaceful than they had any right to be after the day he'd had. Rivers and Croft are in custody. Charles and Ray are in holding. Ortiz was already bargaining for leniency. And yet the silence pressed heavier than noise.

He drove with the window cracked, night air sharp against his jaw, as if the cold might keep his mind from circling the same loop: Rivers' smile, calm, smug, untouched. At home, the loop continued due to hours of interrogation, every question parried, every ledger explained away with language slick enough to pass for reason…still nothing. Rivers hadn't asked for an attorney. He didn't need to. He was his own counsel, his own performance, his own shield.

It was supposed to feel like victory. Instead, it felt like a stalemate. Forty-eight hours. That's all he had before Rivers walked right back into the city like nothing had touched him. Finally, Kramar closed his eyes for the night.

Chapter 23: Unspoken Truths

The next morning, Kramar pulled into St. Central East parking lot. Dawn was just a rumor behind the skyline. He rubbed the fatigue from his eyes, squared his shoulders, and walked through the sliding glass doors.

The ICU had the kind of hush that belonged in a chapel. He passed the nurses' station with a nod, his badge on the lanyard swinging just enough to mark him as belonging. The halls smelled of antiseptic and weak coffee.

Outside Room 314, he paused. Then he eased the door open and lingered in the threshold.

Keith Forest sat slouched in a chair by the window, chin tucked to his chest, eyes closed but not asleep. Aunt Robin sat upright, hands folded in her lap like a sentry, her expression lined with exhaustion that refused to bow. Carolina leaned against the bed rail, fingers brushing her brother's hand as if touch alone could call him back.

The monitor hummed its fragile song: rise, fall, rise.

He paused, studying their faces. He'd seen this look in too many waiting rooms, and it never got easier.

Only then did Kramar step farther into the room, letting the door click shut behind him. "Morning," he said softly.

Three pairs of eyes turned toward him.

"You're back," Aunt Robin said, her tone flat but not unkind. "I told you I'd keep you updated," Kramer said. He stopped at the foot of the bed, studying Asher's pale face, the bruises that painted his skin in fading purples and yellows. "There's progress. Not here at the bed…" He gestured toward Asher. "But with the case."

Carolina straightened. "What kind of progress?"

Kramer took a slow breath. This was the part he usually left to prosecutors, not detectives. But these weren't strangers looking for headlines. They were a family waiting in vigil. They deserved more than the silence he'd given them so far.

"We've confirmed who ordered the hit on your brother," he said.

The room sharpened. Even Keith stirred, eyes opening fully now, his voice rough. "Who?"

Kramer met each of their gaze in turn. "We've made an arrest. I can't share names yet, but it's a major development." Carolina's gasp broke the silence. Aunt Robin's lips pressed into a thin line. Keith closed his eyes and exhaled through his nose. "He's in custody," Kramar said. "Picked up yesterday. He's tied to others we already have, and the case is being built. But…" He paused, letting the silence work. "…Asher's recovery still matters. His testimony could be the piece that seals it."

He didn't linger. He knew desperation when it tried to claw up his throat, and he wouldn't let it show here. Instead, he nodded once, then stepped toward the hall. "I'll be outside if you need me." The door clicked softly shut behind him.

Inside, silence stretched a long moment before Aunt Robin broke it.

"So, it's true," she said, her voice low but edged. "He was tied up with something bigger."

Carolina turned on her. "He wasn't tied up. He was targeted."

Aunt Robin shook her head, eyes fixed on Asher's still form. "Don't defend what we both know. That boy's pride made him blind. Someone saw it and used it."

Carolina's jaw tightened. "He's my brother. He was ambitious, not corrupt. He didn't deserve this."

"Ambition without humility becomes corruption," Aunt Robin said. "You don't have to steal money to be stolen yourself. Pride does that just as well."

Keith leaned forward, elbows on his knees, hands clasped. His voice came out raw. "I should have seen it. A father's supposed to know. The hours, the deals too good to be true, the way he smiled like he was on top of the world. I was too proud of him to look harder."

Carolina whirled toward him, eyes bright. "Don't you say that. This isn't your fault. He made choices, yes, but you can't carry his mistakes."

Keith's gaze dropped to his hands. "I carried pride like it was a badge. He learned it from me. Every time I told him I was proud, I never stopped to ask if he was safe. Just if he was successful."

Aunt Robin reached across, resting her hand briefly on his shoulder. "You loved him the best way you knew how. Don't twist that into guilt."

Keith shook his head, voice thick. "Love without caution isn't enough."

Carolina turned back to the bed, gripping Asher's limp hand tighter. "He doesn't need more blame piled on him. He needs us to believe he can wake up. If he opens his eyes and hears nothing but disappointment, what then?"

"He'll hear the truth," Aunt Robin said quietly. "And love. The two can live in the same room."

Carolina's chin lifted stubbornly. "I'll defend him until he can defend himself. He was trying to build something. To prove himself. Maybe he reached too far, but that doesn't make him a criminal. He's not the guy who orders hits on other people."

"No," Aunt Robin said. "He's not. But he walked close enough to the edge that the river nearly swallowed him whole." Her eyes softened. "I don't say this because I don't love him, Lina. I say it because I do. He has to learn that love isn't blind applause."

Carolina blinked rapidly, tears threatening. "You sound like you've already given up on him."

"I haven't," Aunt Robin said firmly. "But I won't lie to myself or to him when he wakes. He needs honesty more than he needs excuses."

Keith rose, pacing to the window. The sunlight gazed through the window. His shoulders sagged. "When he was a boy, I told myself he was different. Special. That kind of pride… it felt good. But maybe I was teaching him the wrong lesson. Maybe I was teaching him that falling was something other men did."

He pressed his forehead briefly against the glass. "If I could trade places with him, I would."

Carolina crossed to him, touching his arm. "We don't need trades, Dad. We need him awake."

The three of them fell into silence again, broken only by the steady beep of the monitor. Each carried their own truth: Keith's guilt, Robin's disappointment, Carolina's fierce defense.

Finally, Aunt Robin spoke, her voice was gentler now. "Whatever comes out when he wakes, answers, excuses, confessions, it won't erase the fact that he's ours. Family doesn't vanish because pride bruises it. We'll face the truth together."

Carolina nodded, tears slipping free. "Then let him wake. Let him tell us himself."

Keith turned from the window, eyes rimmed red. He looked at his son, still and pale, and whispered, "Come back, Asher. Not for me. Not for pride. For the truth."

The monitor kept its rhythm, indifferent, but in the room, three people leaned closer, each carrying questions only he could answer.

Outside the door, Kramar spoke quietly into his phone with the ADA's office, his voice low, his words clipped: strategy, warrants, next steps. He was building a case brick by brick.

But the ADA's tone on the other end carried no triumph. Without a testimony from the victim, we're thin, she said. Fraud, maybe. Conspiracy at best. But murder? Disappearances? Too much circumstantial, not enough hard evidence.

Kramar closed his eyes, pressing a hand to the bridge of his nose. He'd heard this song before, a case slipping through the cracks because the one voice that mattered most was silent.

We can't hold him any longer. He'll be released today, the ADA finished.

The call ended. The glow of his phone dimmed in his palm. "Rivers is walking free."

Kramar slid the phone into his pocket, jaw set. "Hold on, kid," he muttered under his breath. "Because without you, he keeps running this city with the same deceitful tactics."

Inside Room 314, machines carried Asher's fragile rhythm. The family waited for a different kind of testimony, the kind only Asher could give. Carolina smoothed the sheet near his arm, whispering more to herself than to anyone else. "If you could just open your eyes, we'd know the truth."

Aunt Robin's gaze lingered on his battered face. "The truth has a way of showing itself, whether we want it or not."

The monitor kept time, steady and unbroken. But beneath its rhythm, the truth was already waiting buried in memory, hidden in hours no one in this room had seen.

And it began on the night Asher thought he was untouchable.

Chapter 24: The Beating

This was how it began, the night that brought him here, the night that left him broken in a hospital bed.

The city had long since gone quiet, but Asher Forest was still in his office, hunched over the glow of two monitors. His tie was loose, his jacket slung across the back of his chair. A cold cup of coffee sat forgotten at his elbow, a thin film hardening on its surface.

He barely noticed the ache in his neck, the hour crawling past midnight, or the silence pressing down on the empty building.

Lines of code streamed across the screen, numbers and symbols blurring together, pulling him deeper, pulling him away from the world that waited just outside. Every keystroke brought him closer to the program he believed would change the city. A new system would be streamlined, efficient, and elegant, set to be unveiled at the Civic Data Summit next week. It wasn't just software; it was salvation. With this deal, he could finally prove himself, finally silence the critics, finally pay off Rivers, and close the book on his debts.

In his mind, it was simple: land the contract, get the city's money, and Rivers wouldn't call his goonies. One last gamble. One last performance.

He never noticed the faint creak of the front door downstairs.

Charles and Ray slipped in like wolves crossing an open field. Charles carried a bat, the polished wood glinting under the low hall lights. Ray flexed his fingers, the glint of steel knuckle rings catching with each step. They didn't rush. They didn't need to.

Asher was too deep in the glow of his monitors, too intoxicated by the idea of winning, to sense the storm creeping closer. The hum of the computer, the rhythmic tapping of his keyboard, the scrolling lines of code, they walled him off from the real world.

It wasn't until the office door banged open that he looked up.

"What the hell?" His eyes widened, startled, as Charles and Ray filled the doorway like a bad dream. "What are you doing here?"

Charles's grin was thin and humorless. "The boss isn't waiting any longer for his money."

Asher shoved back from his desk, heart pounding. "No…listen. I'm finishing this program. Next week, I will present it. I land the contract, and Rivers gets every dime I owe him. He needs to wait a little longer."

Ray's laugh was sharp. "No more waiting."

Before Asher could move, Charles lifted the bat and brought it crashing down on the nearest monitor. Glass exploded in a spray of sparks and shards. The glow that had lit Asher's obsession vanished in an instant.

"No!" Asher lunged from his chair, grabbing at the broken screen. "Why would you do that? That was my work….my computer…you idiot!"

Ray stepped forward fast. The punch came quick and brutal, the steel rings smashing across Asher's jaw. His head snapped back, a burst of pain blinding him white. He hit the floor hard.

Ray bent over him, sneering. "Now who's the idiot?"

Blood filled Asher's mouth. He tried to push himself up, but Charles was already moving, swinging the bat down. The wood slammed into his ribs with a crack that sent fire lancing through his chest. He gasped, the air punched out of him.

"You thought you could outsmart Rivers?" Charles snarled, swinging again. The bat caught Asher's shoulder this time, sending him sprawling. "Well, you didn't. And here's the cost of your arrogance."

Ray's boot connected with his stomach. Another blow came from the bat to his back, arm, and thigh. Each strike tore through his body like lightning, leaving him trembling, gasping, scrambling to crawl away.

"Stop…please…Stop…" His words broke, wet with blood.

The blows didn't stop.

He curled his arms over his head, trying to shield himself, but Charles swung relentlessly, and Ray's fists and boots found every unguarded angle. The office, which had once been a sanctuary, became a cage; the fluorescent lights above buzzed like indifferent witnesses.

Time blurred. The pain was endless, the rhythm of impact unrelenting. He tried to crawl toward the door, but Ray kicked his hand away, stomping down on his wrist until something popped. He screamed, a ragged sound that barely resembled his voice.

Then, suddenly, it was over.

Asher lay on the floor, chest heaving, blood dripping from his mouth, his body a patchwork of agony. His lip was split, his nose leaking warm rivers down his face. His ribs screamed with each shallow breath. His head throbbed worse than any migraine he'd ever known, a pounding drumbeat against his skull.

"Get him up," Charles ordered.

Ray grabbed Asher under the arms, yanking him to his feet. His legs buckled, refusing to hold his weight.

"I can't…" Asher croaked.

"You don't have to," Charles said, slinging him over his shoulder like dead weight.

The world tilted and spun as Charles carried him down the hall. Asher could barely keep his eyes open; every bounce was a new wave of pain. He wanted to scream, to call for help, but his throat was raw, and his voice shredded to nothing.

They hauled him outside into the cold night. The air stung his lungs. He caught a glimpse of the SUV, black and waiting. The trunk yawned open.

"No…" he whispered, shaking his head weakly. "Please…. No…"

They didn't listen. They never would.

Charles and Ray dumped him into the trunk like luggage, the metal floor biting into his broken ribs. The lid slammed shut, plunging him into darkness.

Asher tried to move, but every muscle screamed in protest. He curled onto his side, coughing blood, the sound wet and ragged. Terror clawed at him, sharp and merciless. His chest felt tight, every breath a fight. His thoughts scattered in fragments: I should've paid sooner. I should've walked away. I should've…

The car jolted into motion. Each bump sent pain flaring through his bones. He clenched his teeth, his eyes watering, as he prayed to stay conscious and hoped someone would hear him.

Minutes blurred. Then the SUV slowed and stopped. The trunk creaked open, light stabbing his eyes.

"Out," Charles said.

Asher tried to move, but his body refused. He was too weak, too broken. Ray reached in, grabbed him by the shirt, and hauled him out. His legs dangled uselessly.

Charles hefted him over his shoulder again, carrying him like cargo.

The air grew colder and damper as they descended the concrete steps. The sound of a door opening echoed, hinges groaning. The scent hit him next, a damp stone, mildew, and something metallic that smelled like rust and blood.

The basement.

Asher's head lolled. His vision swam. He felt rope bite into his wrists as they tied him to a chair, the fibers rough and unyielding. His chest heaved shallowly, each breath a struggle. His lip trembled, swollen and bleeding.

He tried to lift his head, to see, but the shadows pressed thick.

Then a voice…low, deliberate, smooth, rose from the darkness.

"Mr. Forest."

The sound froze him more than the ropes did. He didn't need to see the speaker; he knew.

From the far corner, a shadow shifted. Grayson Rivers stepped into the faint light, his suit immaculate, his expression unreadable.

Charles and Ray moved aside.

Asher's heart slammed against his battered ribs.

The king had arrived. "From the far corner, a shadow shifted. Grayson Rivers stepped into the light."

Chapter 25: The Debt

The basement light flickered once, buzzing faintly, then steadied.

Asher lifted his head with effort, blood matting his hair, his breath shallow and uneven. His arms trembled against the ropes binding him to the chair. Every muscle screamed. His chest burned with each inhale, his ribs raw fire. He blinked hard, trying to focus through the haze of pain.

And then he saw him.

Grayson Rivers stepped from the shadows like he'd been waiting there all along. Immaculate suit. Shoes polished enough to catch the dim light. Not a strand of hair out of place. Calm in a way that mocked the chaos around him.

Charles and Ray lingered by the wall, but Rivers raised a hand without looking at them. "Out."

They obeyed without question, their boots heavy on the stairs as they disappeared, the door slamming shut behind them.

Now it was just the two of them.

Rivers approached slowly, his footsteps measured, deliberate. He circled the chair once before stopping directly in front of Asher. He studied him the way a jeweler studies a flawed diamond—not with pity, but with curiosity.

"Asher Forest," Rivers said softly, his voice smooth as silk. "Ambition in a three-piece suit. Pride wrapped in a tie. Tell me, how does it feel now?"

Asher coughed, the motion ripping through his ribs. Blood filled his mouth, dripping down his chin. "I-I had the money coming," he rasped. "One more week. The contract with the city would've covered everything."

Rivers tilted his head slightly, almost like a teacher humoring a student. "Would have. Could have. Dreams, not debts. You think I run an empire on promises?"

"I just needed time."

"You needed humility." Rivers leaned down slightly, his eyes catching Asher's. "And humility doesn't sign checks."

He straightened, beginning to pace again, slow and patient. "Do you know what I admire about you, Asher? You weren't lazy. Laziness is predictable. You were… bold. You believed you could outsmart me. Outplay me. You thought the current would bend for you." He shook his head, faintly amused. "Pride. It's always pride."

Asher forced his head up, defiance sparking faintly through the pain. "I was going to
pay you."

Rivers smiled, but it wasn't kind. "You don't buy time with intentions. You buy it with payment."

He paused by the table where Asher's bloodied tie lay, discarded during the beating. Rivers picked it up between two fingers, examining the fabric. "Mont Printer

Solutions thought they could buy time. A good man. He believed contracts would save him. He vanished. Allership Dynamics followed. Another dreamer. Another ghost." He dropped the tie back onto the table. "Do you know what their mistake was?"

Asher swallowed, his throat raw. "They… they underestimated you."

Rivers' eyes glinted. "No. They overestimated themselves."

He stepped closer again, lowering his voice. "And so did you."

Asher shook his head weakly. "You can't keep doing this. People will notice. Someone will talk."

Rivers chuckled softly, as if the thought were quaint. "People always talk, Mr. Forest. Talk is noise. Money is silence." He leaned closer, his breath calm, controlled. "And I own more silence in this city than anyone."

Asher tried to spit blood at him, but the attempt was pitiful, dribbling down his own chin. "You… won't win forever."

Rivers' smile widened just slightly, like a man indulging a child. "Forever is a fairy tale. I don't need forever. I need it today. And today… You lost."

He circled behind Asher, letting the silence stretch, the sound of his footsteps echoing in the basement. Then his voice came again, almost gentle. "Do you know why I don't raise my voice? Why don't I swing bats or fists?

Because I don't need to. Control isn't in the strike, it's in the certainty."

He leaned down close to Asher's ear, his tone dropping to a whisper. "And right now, you are certain of one thing: I own you."

Asher's body trembled against the ropes, not from fear but from exhaustion. Every word Rivers spoke pressed heavier than any blow.

Finally, Rivers straightened, smoothed his cuffs, and gave a faint shout toward the stairwell.

The door creaked open. Charles and Ray reappeared, stepping back into the basement. Their presence shifted the air instantly, violence hung around them like smoke.

Rivers didn't look at them as he gave the order, his voice calm, casual, businesslike.

"Take him to the pond," Rivers said. "Make sure he remembers who put him there."

Charles's grin spread, cruel and eager. Ray cracked his knuckles, steel glinting under the basement light.

"No…." Asher croaked, his voice barely audible. "Please…NO."

Rivers didn't flinch. He was already turning toward the shadows again, adjusting his cufflinks like the matter was settled, like the words were just another line item in his day.

Charles and Ray untied the ropes, Asher's limp body collapsing between them. They hauled him up, half-dragging, half-carrying him toward the stairs. His head lolled, vision blurring, pain searing through every nerve.

As they reached the door, Asher twisted weakly in their grip, forcing one last glance over his shoulder.

Rivers stood in the corner, perfectly still, perfectly calm, as though the beating, the blood, the broken man meant nothing at all.

The door slammed shut, and darkness swallowed the basement again. And with that, the night rolled toward the pond, the place where everything began. Rivers left the basement without a backward glance, the night air greeting him like an old friend. By the time he slid behind the wheel of his car, the weight of blood and business was already tucked neatly away, folded like a suit he would never wear inside his home.

Chapter 26: The Dinner

The door clicked shut behind him with the softest of sounds, no louder than a sigh. Grayson Rivers slipped his shoes off at the entryway, setting them neatly side by side. The house was warm, lit in soft gold from the dining room chandelier. He could hear laughter…high, unguarded, childish laughter, floating down the hall.

He inhaled once, deeply, as though shedding an entire world with that breath. The chill of the basement, the metallic tang of blood, the weight of Asher Forest's defeat, all of it stayed outside the threshold.

Inside, he was someone else.

"Daddy!"

Two figures thundered toward him from the dining room: Skylar, eight, and Brooklyn, six, their socks skidding across the hardwood. Skylar clutched a plastic dinosaur in one hand; Brooklyn's braid had already come loose from the day's play.

Rivers crouched, arms open. They collided into him, their small bodies pressing against his suit. He laughed, a warm, genuine sound, scooping them both up with ease. "What's this? Dinosaurs and wild hair? Did the jungle move into my house while I was gone?"

Brooklyn giggled, pressing her face into his shoulder. Skylar roared like his toy.

From the dining room, a third voice chimed in: "Grayson, let them breathe."

His wife, Marisol, leaned in the doorway, a smile tugging at her lips. She wore a simple blouse and apron, her hair pulled back. The smell of roasted chicken and herbs clung to her, a comforting counterpoint to the cologne still lingering on his own collar.

He set the children down and crossed the hall, pressing a kiss to her lips. "Evening."

Her hand lingered against his cheek for a moment, her eyes soft. "Evening. Dinner's ready."

The table was already set, plates steaming. The baby monitor sat at the far end, faint static humming through its speaker.

Dinner was noisy in the way all family dinners are: Skylar talking too much, Brooklyn trying to outdo him, and Marisol gently reminding them to eat more than bread. Rivers sat at the head of the table, listening, interjecting with small jokes, nodding at his wife's reminders. He cut his chicken carefully, never raising his voice, never rushing.

When Skylar asked for help with his math homework, Rivers pulled the worksheet closer, adjusting his glasses. "You see this problem here?" he said, pencil poised. "It's not about guessing. It's about finding the pattern. The world runs on patterns. Once you learn that, you can solve anything."

Skylar beamed when he got the answer right.

Brooklyn tugged at Rivers' sleeve. "Daddy, will you read us the story tonight? Not Mommy, you."

"I wouldn't dare say no," Rivers said, smiling.

His phone buzzed once in his pocket. He pulled it out, glanced at the screen, and pressed the side button to silence it.

Marisol raised an eyebrow. "Work?"

"Work doesn't come through this door," Rivers said easily, slipping the phone back into his jacket. "Not at this hour."

After dinner, he carried the plates to the sink while Marisol herded the children toward the bathroom. Brooklyn protested bedtime; Skylar bragged about staying up late. Rivers only chuckled, rolling his sleeves up as he rinsed dishes.

Later, he joined them upstairs.

The children sat cross-legged on their beds, waiting. A worn storybook lay open on the nightstand. Rivers settled between them, one arm around each child, and began to read. His voice shifted for each character, the growl of a wolf, the squeak of a mouse, the deep tones of a king. Brooklyn laughed so hard she nearly toppled backward; Skylar grinned widely, eyes sparkling.

When the story ended, Rivers kissed their foreheads. "Dream well. Tomorrow's another adventure."

The infant fussed down the hall. Rivers moved before Marisol could, slipping quietly into the nursery. He lifted his youngest from the crib, cradling the small, warm body against his chest.

"Shh," he murmured, rocking gently. He hummed, low and steady, until the cries softened.

Bath time came next. He knelt by the tub, rolling up his sleeves, and washed the baby with slow, careful motions. He spoke softly as he worked, narrating each step as though the infant could understand. "One day, you'll run through the hall with your brother and sister. One day, you'll climb trees. But tonight, we rest. Tonight, we keep the world away."

When the bath was done, he wrapped the baby in a soft towel, gently drying each small hand and each tiny foot. He carried the child back to the nursery, settled into the rocking chair, and fed him from a bottle. The baby's eyes drooped, lids heavy with sleep. Rivers rocked slowly, his expression tender.

When the bottle was empty, he kissed the infant's forehead and laid him gently back in the crib.

Downstairs, the house had gone quiet. Dishes were done, lights dimmed. Rivers poured a glass of wine, swirling it once before setting it untouched on the counter. He stared out the kitchen window at the dark yard beyond, hands steady, expression unreadable.

His phone buzzed again, vibrating against the counter. He turned it face down without looking.

When he finally went upstairs, Marisol was waiting in bed, lamp casting a warm glow across the room. She watched him slide beneath the covers, her smile weary but full of affection.

"You didn't take a single call," she said softly.

"I told you," he replied. "Work stays outside."

She brushed her fingers over his arm. "How was your day, honey?"

Rivers turned his head toward her. In the soft light, his eyes gave nothing away. A small smile tugged at the corner of his mouth.

"Just business," he said.

The lamp clicked off. The room fell into darkness. In the dark, he lay still, his breathing even, as if the night had asked nothing more of him. But the city remembered. And while Grayson Rivers lay in his own bed, the weight of blood was tucked neatly away as if it were nothing more than business. While Asher Forest lay broken at Great Pond, unseen, unheard, the night held its secret tight.

But secrets never last. By dawn, the city would know his name again.

Chapter 27: The Table of Regrets

More than a week ago, Asher Forest had been pulled from the water and was now clinging to life in this place of machines and monitors. The beating was over. The waiting had begun.

The hallway smelled of antiseptic and stale coffee that had been there for hours. Kramer pressed his phone back into his pocket, the call with the ADA still echoing in his head. His pulse had slowed from the interrogation room's intensity, but his mind hadn't stopped moving.

The hospital felt different at night, quieter, heavier. The fluorescent lights buzzed overhead, their hum mixing with the occasional squeak of sneakers on tile. A nurse wheeled a cart past him, nodding politely, and disappeared through double doors.

Kramer rubbed the bridge of his nose, exhaling.

The elevator at the far end opened, and a man in a white coat stepped out. Middle-aged, glasses low on his nose, a clipboard tucked under his arm. Kramer caught him before he could move past.

"Doctor."

The man paused, eyes flicking to Kramer's badge. "Detective. You're here late."

"I'm here for Asher Forest," Kramer said. "Can you give me an update?"

The doctor adjusted his glasses, posture tightening with the practiced caution of someone who had given this speech too many times. "Mr. Forest is in critical condition. Stable for the moment, but the injuries are severe."

"I need specifics," Kramer pressed.

The doctor shook his head slightly. "You're not immediate family. Privacy laws restrict what I can say."

Kramer exhaled sharply. "You've got to give me something. Anything."

The man hesitated, then softened, lowering his voice. "Internal bleeding. Multiple fractures. Severe head trauma. He's… fragile. We're doing what we can."

Kramer nodded, jaw tight. "That's enough."

The doctor offered a polite but distant look before stepping away.

Kramer leaned against the wall, staring down the hall toward Asher's room. Through the small window, he could see Keith slumped in a chair, Carolina perched on the edge of the bed, Aunt Robin with her hands folded, lips moving in prayer.

The monitor beeped steadily for now.

Kramer rubbed his temples. He couldn't shake Rivers' face from the interrogation room, couldn't shake the calm certainty that came with every word the man spoke. He needed Asher. He needed him to wake up.

A sudden rush of motion broke the stillness. A nurse sprinted past, nearly clipping Kramer's shoulder. Another followed, pushing a crash cart.

The intercom crackled to life: "Code Blue. Room 314. Code Blue."

Asher's room.

Kramer shoved off the wall, heart kicking. Through the glass, he saw the monitor flatline, the long, merciless beep filling the hall. Nurses swarmed. A doctor barked orders. Keith stumbled back, his face white. Carolina cried out. Aunt Robin clutched the chair, whispering louder now, her prayer turning urgent.

Kramer pressed his hand against the glass, helpless to move closer.

Inside, chaos reigned. Electrodes ripped free. The crash cart's paddles came alive. "Charging!" someone shouted. The defibrillator whined. Asher's body jolted once, then slumped.

"Again!"

Another charge. Another jolt.

No rhythm.

Kramer felt his throat go dry. The detective in him wanted to catalog the scene, but the man in him tried to smash through the door and wake Asher. He stayed rooted to the spot.

Inside the room, the doctor's voice cut through: "Prepare to call it."

At the Table…..And then, silence.

Not in the room. Not in the hall. Inside Asher himself.

He opened his eyes to a place he didn't know but somehow recognized.

A long wooden table stretched before him, smooth and polished, lit by a light that seemed to come from nowhere. On the table lay objects, scattered like evidence in a case he couldn't escape: a whiskey glass, a set of dice, a shredded contract, a blood-stained shirt, a gleaming coin. Each one pulsed faintly, glowing with memory.

Asher lowered his head, heart heavy. He knew what each object was. He knew what each one meant.

He was not alone.

Across from him, a figure sat neither man nor woman, young nor old. Its presence filled the space with a weight that pressed into Asher's chest. The voice, when it came, was clear and unyielding, resonant as if spoken both aloud and within.

"Asher Forest," it said. "You have reached the table of your regrets. Every choice, every path, every moment you believed you were untouchable has led you here."

Asher's hands trembled. He tried to speak, but no words came.

The figure's voice continued, steady and piercing:

"Let us walk honestly, as in the day; not in rioting and drunkenness, not in chambering and wantonness, not in strife and envying. But put ye on the Lord Jesus Christ, and make not provision for the flesh, to fulfil the lusts thereof."

Romans 13:13-14 KJV

The words struck him like blows. Images flashed around the table, nights in clubs, laughter spilling with liquor, dice rattling against felt tables, women whose names he never remembered. Business deals are struck not with honesty, but with arrogance.

Asher lowered his head, shame burning his skin.

The voice spoke again:

"Whose end is destruction, whose God is their belly, and whose glory is in their shame, who mind earthly things."

Philippians 3:19 KJV

The table was filled with more visions, his hand reaching for another man's company, justifying it as a strategy. His mouth shaped words of flattery to judges and council members, twisting truth into something useful. His heart swelled with pride when crowds laughed at his insults, when contracts bowed to his will.

He groaned, pressing his hands against his face. "I was wrong," he whispered. "All of it…. I was wrong."

The figure leaned closer, voice still even:

"You clothed yourself in pride and called it genius. You filled yourself with excess and called it living. You built an altar to yourself and called it success."

Asher shook, his shoulders trembling. "I don't want this anymore. It was too much."

Silence fell heavy across the table. Then the voice came one last time, firm and final:

"And if it seem evil unto you to serve the Lord, choose you this day whom ye will serve; whether the gods which your fathers served that were on the other side of the flood, or the gods of the Amorites, in whose land ye dwell: but as for me and my house, we will serve the Lord."

Joshua 24:15 KJV

The words cut through him, dividing past from future.

A choice.

The table glowed brighter, papers floating in the air, objects trembling. One path stretched into shadow: chaos, destruction, ruin. The other shone faintly, narrow but steady.

Asher closed his eyes, tears streaking his battered face. His voice quivered.

"I will serve the Lord. I choose Him."

The figure nodded once. Its voice softened, almost tender.

"Then wake up."

Back in the Room, the defibrillator whined again, the paddles pressing against Asher's chest.

"Clear!"

The shock jolted him. For a moment, nothing. Then…

A gasp. Ragged, broken, desperate.

Asher's chest heaved, pulling in air like a drowning man breaking the surface. His eyes shot open, unfocused but alive.

"Got a pulse!" a nurse shouted. The monitor beeped erratically, then steadied into rhythm.

Keith stumbled forward, tears spilling. Aunt Robin dropped to her knees, hands raised in trembling gratitude. Carolina cried openly, clutching her brother's limp hand.

Kramer exhaled, his shoulders sagging. He pressed a palm against the door, watching as the doctors moved quickly, stabilizing, securing, shouting orders of relief instead of surrender.

As the room settled into a fragile semblance of normalcy, the monitor kept time again… not indifferent now, but insistent.

Asher Forest had made his choice.

And for the first time since the night the city swallowed him, he was grateful.

Chapter 28: Aftermath

The room had finally become quieter after the storm of Code Blue. The crash cart was wheeled out. The doctors spoke in low tones, their hands steady, their eyes sharp. The monitor now beat a rhythm again, thin and fragile, but it was there.

Asher lay still, his chest rising shallow but steady. His skin was pale, his lips cracked, his eyes half-closed in the light.

Keith stood closest, gripping the rail of the bed so hard his knuckles whitened. He hadn't moved since the last jolt that brought his son back. His face was lined with something more than exhaustion; it was guilt, deep and old, etched into him like weather into stone.

Carolina clung to Asher's hand, her thumb brushing over the IV tape, whispering words no one else could hear. Her tears hadn't stopped, though now they fell softer, slower.

Aunt Robin sat with her Bible in her lap, her thumb pressed into the worn leather, her lips still moving, though the urgency of her prayer had shifted into gratitude.

Kramer lingered near the doorway. He didn't intrude, didn't offer words. His badge carried weight, but in this room it meant nothing. He watched, his arms folded, silent but steady. The detective in him catalogued vitals, noted the medical staff's expressions, and tracked every small sign. The man in him, though, felt something heavier. Relief.

The lead doctor finally stepped closer to Keith, his voice calm but firm. "He's stable for now. However, please note that this is not considered recovery. He's still very weak. We don't know the extent of his neurological function yet."

Keith swallowed hard. "But he's alive."

"Yes," the doctor said, with the measured patience of someone who'd seen too many families cling to the word. "Alive. His body responded. That's a start."

"Will he talk?" Carolina asked quickly, her eyes hopeful.

The doctor shook his head gently. "Coming out of a coma is not like waking from sleep. It's gradual. Right now, he may open his eyes, track movement, maybe squeeze a hand. You shouldn't expect conversation yet. His brain and body need time to adjust."

Aunt Robin nodded, as though she already knew. "The Lord gives in His time. Not ours."

Keith's grip on the bedrail tightened. He looked at Asher's face, bruised and still, tubes and tape obscuring the features he'd once celebrated at graduations and parties. "I should've seen it," he muttered, his voice low. "All those late nights, the missed calls. I should've known something was wrong."

Carolina turned sharply. "This isn't your fault, Dad."

Keith didn't look at her. His eyes stayed on his son. "Fathers are supposed to know."

"Sisters are supposed to defend, too," Carolina whispered, her hand squeezing Asher's. "And I'll keep doing it until he can speak for himself."

Robin closed her Bible, setting it gently on the bedside table. "Keith, guilt won't heal him. Love might. Prayer surely will. But guilt? That only binds you the same way pride bound him."

Her words sat heavy in the room.

Kramer shifted slightly, letting the family have the space. His chest loosened for the first time in hours. He wouldn't show it, but inside he felt a surge of relief so sharp it almost startled him. Asher had survived. That meant there was still a chance. For justice. For testimony. For truth.

But he didn't smile. He didn't speak. He just let the family cling to what they needed most: each other.

Hours bled into the late night. Nurses came and went, checking vitals, adjusting IV drips, shining small lights into Asher's eyes. He didn't stir. His breathing remained shallow but steady, the ventilator helping to regulate the rhythm.

Carolina hadn't left his side. She kept whispering, sometimes nonsense, sometimes memories, sometimes just his name.

"Remember when we got caught sneaking out of Aunt Robin's house?" she whispered, tears glinting. "You told Dad it was all you, that I just followed. You saved me then, Asher. I'll save you now. Just come back."

Keith finally sank into a chair, his shoulders hunched, staring at his son. His eyes were red, but he wouldn't let the tears fall. He'd carried pride for so long, it was hard to set it down, even here.

Robin sat quietly, hands folded in her lap, her silence heavier than words.

Kramer stepped out into the hall, pulling the door quietly closed. He leaned against the wall, running a hand down his face. The precinct, the files, the interrogations…all of it felt a world away. He didn't let himself think of victory often. It was dangerous. But tonight, he allowed himself one breath of it.

Asher Forest was alive.

The hours stretched. Midnight passed. Two nurses entered quietly to reposition Asher, adjusting the pillows to prevent pressure sores and turning him slightly to aid his breathing. Carolina helped, guiding his limp arm back onto the sheet. She didn't flinch at the bruises, nor did she look away from the swelling.

A faint sound came then. Small, weak, but real.

Asher's throat moved. His lips parted, a rasp of air slipping through. His eyes fluttered, then opened halfway.

Carolina gasped. "Dad…. Aunt Robin…look!"

Keith bolted upright. Robin leaned forward, her Bible sliding to the floor unnoticed.

"Asher," Carolina whispered, leaning close. "It's me. It's Lina. Can you hear me?"

His eyes shifted, slowly, heavy, like dragging anchors through water. But they found her. They saw her.

Her tears came harder. "That's it. That's my brother."

Keith reached forward, his hand shaking as he brushed the edge of Asher's arm. "Son…"

Asher's mouth moved, but no sound came. His throat strained, only a dry rasp escaping. His eyes fluttered closed again, exhausted from the effort.

The doctor appeared quickly, checking the monitors and nodding once. "This is good. Eye movement, recognition. He's responding. Don't push him to speak. His body needs rest. Talking will come later."

Carolina nodded, still holding Asher's hand, her thumb stroking across his knuckles.

Robin's voice trembled as she whispered, "Thank You, Lord."

Keith lowered into the chair again, covering his face with his hands. The sound that escaped him was half sob, half sigh.

Kramer returned quietly, standing in the doorway. He saw it…the faintest squeeze of Asher's hand, the flicker of his eyes, the minor miracle that he was still here.

The detective in him calculated how long it would take to ask questions and how long it would take to gather testimony. But for tonight, he didn't need answers.

For tonight, it was enough that Asher Forest was alive.

Kramer leaned his shoulder against the doorframe, watching the family draw closer around the bed. He let the corners of his mouth twitch upward, just once. Not for them to see. Just for himself.

It wasn't a victory. Not yet. But it was hope.

Chapter 29: Marble and Glass

By morning, Asher was stable, his family still keeping vigil. Kramer carried that fragile hope with him as he walked into Rivers' world of marble and glass.

The tower wore its morning like polished armor. Sun flooded through the glass façade, sliced into ribbons by steel. The marble lobby gleamed. Security badges beeped at waist-high turnstiles, the sound neat and civilized; the elevator banks swallowed men and women in tailored suits and rereleased them onto floors humming with quiet purpose. On the wall behind the concierge desk, a brushed-metal logo spelled the name that opened doors and closed mouths: RIVERS.

Kramer arrived with two uniforms and Detective Velez, who never smiled on weekdays. The warrant sat in the inner pocket of his jacket like a heartbeat he didn't trust. He flashed his badge at security and watched the concierge's expression tilt from routine courtesy toward dread.

"Is there… a problem, Detective?" the man asked, already knowing the answer.

"Elevator," Kramer said. "Top floor."

They rode in silence. The car's walls showed them back to themselves: distortions in steel, faces stretched a little thinner than the morning should allow. Kramer checked his phone once. A single line from the charge nurse at St. Central East: Open eyes, following simple commands.

Stable. He didn't reply. He just let the words settle where they belonged—between relief and resolve.

The doors parted onto a floor of frost-white carpet and quiet money. A receptionist with immaculate bangs rose halfway out of her chair, confusion throwing shadows behind her eyes.

"Good morning," she began, then stopped when she saw the uniforms. "Do you have an appointment?"

"We have a warrant," Velez said, and placed it flat on the desk like a card no one else had been allowed to play.

The receptionist's gaze flicked involuntarily toward the glass office at the far end of the hall. The door was open. Sunlight poured across a walnut desk cleared to surgical precision. Grayson Rivers stood with his back to the view, speaking softly to a man whose posture suggested expensive legal training and a lifelong love of billable hours.

When Rivers lifted his head, he saw Kramer first. The faintest recognition passed across his face—no surprise, no anger, just the calm of a man who'd considered this scene in advance and decided it would look better with his chin level.

The lawyer turned, nostrils flaring. "Detective, you can't...."

"We can," Kramer said. He didn't raise his voice. He didn't need to. "Grayson Rivers, you're under arrest for conspiracy to commit assault, witness intimidation, fraud, and obstruction of justice. Additional charges pending."

Rivers' expression didn't change. He closed the folder on his desk with a fingertip, glanced at the lawyer once, the kind of glance that moves money, and then looked back at Kramer.

"I assume this means you finally found someone willing to say my name on record," he said mildly.

"We did," Kramer said. He took one step closer, close enough to see his own reflection in Rivers' polished cufflink. He lowered his voice so only the two of them could hear. "He's awake."

For the first time since Kramer had known him, something small and human crossed Rivers' face, a tightening at the corner of the jaw so slight you could mistake it for a trick of light. He smoothed it away with a blink.

"Congratulations," Rivers said. "On your patient's improved health."

"Turn around," Kramer said.

The lawyer's voice sharpened. "This is theatre. My client is a respected businessman. He will appear voluntarily. There is no need for…."

Cuffs.

Velez stepped in with the practiced efficiency of someone who believed in steel more than promises. Rivers didn't resist. He turned as requested and presented his wrists like a gentleman putting on a watch.

In the outer office, heads began to lift. The whisper moved through the open floor plan the way heat moves through thin air: sudden, everywhere. Staffers rose from their chairs. Phones went slack in mid-air. Someone said "What?" too loudly. A woman near the glass wall pressed her hands to her mouth and looked as though she wanted to run but couldn't remember where to.

Kramer let the lawyer talk at his shoulder as they guided Rivers through the door. They stepped into the corridor, past framed photos of ribbon cuttings and charity galas, and into a world that Rivers had built, a world of life where kitchens were stocked with almonds and glossy magazines, and all-hands meetings were held where the words "culture" and "family" were spoken like blessings.

"Mr. Rivers?" a young man blurted, stepping too close. He wore a company hoodie over a button-down, loyalty layered like clothing. "Sir, what's happening?"

Rivers angled his head toward him and offered a small, composed smile that made two women near the copier visibly exhale.

"It's a misunderstanding, Evan," he said. "Focus on your work."

"But, this is harassment," someone else said, anger blooming where fear had been. "He gives half this city a paycheck. You can't just…."

Velez's gaze flicked over the crowd: marketing, operations, legal, janitorial… each face a version of the same belief. Respect wasn't just admiration; it was cover. It made a man like Rivers look more like an institution than a person.

"Back up," the taller uniform said, hand open, not unkind. "Give us space."

They moved anyway. A handful followed into the elevator lobby, voices rising in the way voices do when they want to make reality back up by volume.

"He donates to the school district."

"He paid for my mom's surgery when our insurance was canceled."

"He built the scholarship fund for underserved children."

"He doesn't deserve."

"Why are you doing this?"

Kramer worked the cuffs like a metronome. He didn't turn to address the crowd; he addressed the man wearing them. "You have the right to remain silent. Anything you say can and will…"

The lawyer cut across. "He's invoking."

Rivers didn't open his mouth to say he was. He let the attorney's sentence hang like a veil.

Kramer finished the Miranda anyway. The procedure wasn't for the man in cuffs. It was for the record.

The elevator dinged. The doors slid open. No one got on. No one got off. The lobby hummed with outrage calibrated to be heard and gratitude calibrated to look like courage.

As the doors began to close, a woman with a lanyard and an expression like carved stone stepped forward and hit the button with her palm. HR, Kramer guessed. Or a senior VP whose inbox was now an emergency.

"This is wrong," she said. She didn't raise her voice; she didn't need to. She looked directly at Kramer, past the badge, the way you look past a tool to the hand holding it. "You don't parade a man through his company like this."

Kramer held her gaze. He could see, behind the precision of her eyeliner, a ledger of things Rivers had paid for—bonuses, maternity leave supplements, a fruit basket sent when her father died. He could also see the thing she couldn't: a basement, a chair, a command given in a voice that never needed to shout.

"What we're doing," he said evenly, "is this necessary."

"For whom?" she asked.

"For the truth."

The elevator took them down to the lobby like a throat swallowing. The doors opened onto a room that had rearranged itself in thirty seconds: security radios crackling, the concierge on the phone saying the sentence you only ever want to say once, bystanders doing the math of whether they were close enough to be witnesses but far enough to say they weren't.

They crossed the marble. Rivers' shoes were gone— surrendered at the threshold to the courtesy of his home and now to the courtesy of the law. He moved barefoot on stone and didn't wince. A camera flash popped somewhere near the revolving door, the sound obscene in a morning that had been ordinary.

"Mr. Rivers!" a voice called from behind the rope line that building management had produced with astonishing speed. "Are you being targeted because of your political donations?"

"Is this about the hospital?" another voice shouted, hunger sharpening it.

Rivers kept walking. He didn't turn his head. He didn't do anything as small as pretending not to hear. He existed, centered inside a life that had trained itself not to flinch.

At the curb, the cruiser waited, its lights off, engine idling low. The uniforms opened the back door. Rivers paused—not to resist, not to glare, but to give himself one last look at the front of the building that bore his name. You could choose to read it as sentiment. You could choose to read it as inventory. He got in.

Kramer leaned an arm on the roof and looked back into the lobby. The elevator banks had become a gallery. Employees stared from behind glass like aquarium fish watching a storm form over their ocean. Fear, outrage, and confusion, none of them added up to knowledge.

He bent and spoke through the open door to the man in the back seat. "He's awake," he said again, not to taunt, not to gloat. To inform.

Rivers' gaze didn't flicker this time. If anything, his pupils contracted. He was a man to whom information was a temperature set by a dial only he could see. He said nothing.

The door shut with a soft, domestic sound. A few people outside flinched anyway.

"Let's move," Velez told the driver.

They pulled out into the traffic that belonged to everyone, not just men with their names on buildings. The cruiser merged into a lane where a courier cut them off, and a bus sighed at a red light like a pensioner. The tower receded in the mirror, then became a slice of glass, then became the kind of thing you can pretend you never saw.

Kramer let the silence stand for a block. He watched Rivers's reflection in the plexiglass partition, his calm profile visible, jaw set, the cuff chain catching a spot of sun and throwing it back in a little arc.

"You could help yourself," Kramer said, not bothering to turn. "You know that." The lawyer's voice crackled over the speakerphone resting on the front seat. He wasn't there in person, but his tone carried the same weight. "Detective, my client won't be answering questions. You're trying to trap him with words, and we're not playing that game."

"Good," Kramer said. "I prefer facts."

In the rearview, Rivers smiled. It was smaller than most smiles, and it didn't reach his eyes. His voice, when he finally used it, was gentle.

"Facts," he said. "Like the kind that told you last time you couldn't hold me."

"That was then," Kramer said.

"And this is now," Rivers agreed, as if they were discussing weather patterns.

The driver took a left. Sirens stayed off. There was no need to announce what gravity could do by itself.

Back at the office, without the weight of the man who made the weight of the place, the floor did what living things do when they've been startled: it tried to find its rhythm again. It failed.

The receptionist sat very still, her hands folded so tightly the knuckles were white, as if holding on could keep the morning from finishing its sentence. Two junior analysts stood in the space just beyond her desk, speaking in voices that had dropped from indignation to pleading.

"He pays for the birthday cake every month."

"He sent flowers when my mom was in the ICU."

"He flew to Phoenix to be at the ribbon cutting; he didn't have to…"

"He knows my kid's name."

"It's a mistake," the receptionist said, over and over, to them or to herself.

Across the open office, a man in a blazer, his expression one of worry, stood on a chair and tried to be a leader.

"Everyone, please," he said. "Back to work. Legal will handle this. We do what we've always done, our jobs."

No one moved for a beat. Then a handful did. A handful didn't.

By the window, a woman cried softly and typed something into a social feed.

Thirty screens lit up thirty seconds later: *Is he okay? Does anyone know what's happening?*

HR sent an email that began: We *know this isn't easy* and ended with *'Take the rest of the morning if you need it.'*

The legal team left their glass cube and disappeared into an interior room with the blinds pulled down, which made it feel illegal even if it wasn't. Security revised their protocols.

The man from facilities stared at the door. Kramer had walked through and called a contractor to discuss the weight tolerance of the hinges.

By the time the first reporter made it into the lobby with a microphone and a smile that had been rehearsed in cars at more scenes like this than should exist, the elevator doors could no longer be trusted to open onto anything other than a smaller world.

On the street, the cruiser turned onto an avenue that became a cross street, which in turn became a block where the courthouse would one day be mentioned in a sentence that included the word 'history'. The city passed by outside: a woman with a stroller and a coffee, a man hauling twelve cases of bottled water, a boy who looked like Asher at a safe age, running for a bus he'd make even if he didn't need to.

Kramer's phone buzzed. He glanced down: Forest resting. Responded to the name. No speech yet. He put the phone face down on his knee. He needed to compartmentalize, too. Just differently.

He thought of Aunt Robin's hand on the blanket, of Keith swallowing his guilt as if it were something with edges, of Carolina's thumb tracing the line of tape on her brother's wrist. He thought of how quiet the room had gone when the monitor found its rhythm again. He thought of a basement, a pond, and a man who said Just business, like it was weather.

"You chose this," he said, not to Rivers but to the air. Maybe to himself.

Rivers watched the city slide by. "We all do," he said, voice mild. "That's what makes it fair."

Velez snorted softly. She had a way of telling the truth with her nose. "Fair," she said. "That's a new word for it."

They rolled through another light. A cyclist tapped the trunk with an open palm to make a point about space and didn't realize he had just touched a story his fingerprints would never match.

At the precinct, the lot had vacancies, which meant it was too early for the press to have guessed which door mattered. Velez nosed the cruiser into a spot near the side entrance. The uniforms climbed out, opened the back door, and did what gravity does in human form: they brought a man from one box into another.

Inside the interview corridor, the fluorescent hum was the same every day, ending with paperwork. A custodian pushed a cart slowly as if not to scare the dust. Someone down the hall laughed at something that had nothing to do with justice and everything to do with surviving a job.

Kramer took Rivers' arm, neither roughly nor gently, and guided him to Interview Room Four. The same room. The same table. The camera's red light blinked its little metronome of time passing.

The lawyer caught up, breathless with indignation and the kind of fitness that sits on a schedule rather than a treadmill. He slapped a folder on the table as if sound could file motions.

"My client is saying nothing," he announced.

"Good," Kramer said. "It's my turn."

He placed a single page on the table and turned it so Rivers could read it. It wasn't a confession. It wasn't a ledger. It was a hospital form, the kind that showed a name printed plainly where it mattered and a status written not in code but in a word: Awake.

Rivers' gaze slid over it like water over glass. "How is his family?" he asked, as if the question were compassion rather than reconnaissance.

"They're present," Kramer said.

"How nice," Rivers murmured.

Kramer sat. He didn't open a file. He didn't start with questions.

He let the room be small. He let the idea be large.

He thought of how many times men had mistaken patience for mercy and discovered they were not synonyms.

He thought of the sentence he had said twice already that day and how saying it a third time felt like making the truth true through repetition.

"He's awake," he said again, mostly to himself this time.

Rivers met his eyes, and for a moment, they were two men who knew what sentences could do. Then the lawyer cleared his throat, and the spell broke, and the day returned to its job.

Down on the street, a delivery truck double-parked, making ten men late for ten meetings. On the tower floor, a woman wrote the company-wide email twice but sent neither version. In a hospital room, a man who had thought himself inevitable drifted toward sleep he had chosen to keep.

And in a small, bright room with a camera in the corner, a detective who had learned the difference between patience and surrender set his watch by a single fact and prepared to try again.

Chapter 30: The First Word

Morning crept into the room through blinds half-closed against the night. The light was thin, gray at first, then touched with gold as the sun climbed higher. The monitors hummed their steady song, a fragile rhythm that had become the family's clock.

Keith sat in the chair closest to the bed, his head bent forward, chin nearly touching his chest. He had not meant to fall asleep. His hand was still curled against the rail, as if he'd been holding on even in his dreams.

Aunt Robin dozed in the corner, Bible open in her lap, glasses slipping down her nose. Carolina had slumped sideways on the couch, her brother's hoodie balled under her head as a makeshift pillow.

The room was quiet, only the soft hiss of oxygen and the faint shuffle of feet from the hallway breaking it.

Then, like a stone dropped into still water, a sound stirred the silence.

"…Hi… Dad."

It was hoarse, weak, but unmistakable.

Keith's head snapped up. For a second, he thought he'd dreamed it. But when he looked, he saw his son's eyes open, hazy and heavy, blinking against the light. His lips trembled as though the effort of forming two small words had cost him everything.

"Asher?" Keith's voice cracked. He lurched forward, nearly knocking the chair over. "Son?"

Carolina shot upright, hair in disarray, eyes wide. "What? What is it?"

"He spoke," Keith whispered, stunned. His hand clutched the rail as though afraid the moment might slip through his fingers. "He said… he said hi."

Carolina scrambled to her feet, leaning over the bed. "Asher? Can you see me? It's me…It's Lina."

Asher's gaze shifted slowly, laboriously, until it found her. The faintest curve touched his lips. "Lina…" he breathed, barely audible.

Carolina let out a sob that turned into laughter. She pressed her forehead against his hand, tears sliding freely. "You're back. Oh my God, you're back."

Aunt Robin jerked awake at the commotion. She blinked, adjusting her glasses, then rose quickly when she saw what was happening. Her hand went to her mouth. "Praise the Lord," she whispered, voice trembling. "Praise His holy name."

Keith leaned closer, his face awash with disbelief and something more profound shame wrapped tight around love. "I'm here, son," he said, his hand trembling as it brushed lightly against Asher's arm. "I'm right here."

Asher's eyes flickered with effort, his breath shallow. "Hi… Dad."

Keith broke then, a sob tearing through him. He bowed his head against the rail, shoulders shaking. For months, pride had been the shell he'd lived in. In two words, his son had cracked it wide open.

Carolina reached across the bed, gripping Keith's shoulder. "He's here, Dad. He's really here."

Robin stood over them both, tears streaking down her cheeks, her hands raised heavenward. "Thank You, Lord. Thank you for one more chance."

The doctor entered moments later, drawn by the sudden flurry. He checked the monitors, leaned close with his penlight, and nodded. "Good," he said softly. "Very good. He's responding. Keep the stimulation low. Don't overwhelm him."

Carolina nodded eagerly, brushing her brother's hair gently back from his forehead. "We won't."

Keith sat back down, still gripping the rail as though it anchored him. His son's eyes were open, watching him, hazy but present. That was enough to make his heart pound against his ribs.

It was mid-morning when Kramer arrived. His tie was loose, his face drawn from the long night, but his stride was steady. He paused at the doorway when he saw Asher awake, saw the family gathered close. Something in his chest loosened.

"You're all still here," he said quietly.

Robin turned, her eyes wet but bright. "Where else would we be?"

Kramer stepped closer, his gaze falling on the bed. Asher's eyes tracked him faintly. His lips parted, but no words came this time, just the effort.

"He knows us," Carolina said, her voice fierce with pride. "He knows all of us."

Kramer gave a slight nod, then straightened. He glanced at Keith. "I need to tell you something."

Keith frowned. "Now?"

"Yes," Kramer said. His voice was steady and professional, but softer than usual. "It can't wait."

The family tensed, bracing themselves.

Kramer drew in a slow breath. "We arrested a person in connection with your son's incident this morning. He's in custody."

For a beat, the room froze. Then Carolina let out a cry of relief, her head dropping onto Asher's hand. Robin's hands went up again, whispering another prayer. Keith leaned back in his chair, closing his eyes. His shoulders sagged as if a weight had been lifted he hadn't realized he was still carrying.

Asher's eyes shifted. His chest rose and fell unevenly, a soft sound escaping, half sigh, half sob. His lips shaped one fragile word: "Good."

Carolina kissed his knuckles. "It's over, Ash. It's over."

Kramer didn't correct her. He let the hope stand.

The family didn't press for details. They already knew pieces; there had been men involved, someone pulling strings, even a possible intruder disguised as a nurse. But the whole picture hadn't yet been spoken aloud. What mattered now wasn't evidence or files. What mattered was Asher breathing, Asher seeing, Asher speaking. Keith's hand still held the rail, his thumb brushing unconsciously along the metal. He wanted to ask why, wanted to demand answers from his son, but one look at the pale face on the pillow silenced him. Love spoke louder than blame.

Robin's heart ached with disappointment, but her love was stronger still. She whispered scriptures under her breath, promises she'd prayed over Asher since he was a child.

Carolina sat closest, her grip on his hand unshakable, daring anyone to try to pull her away.

The room was thick with relief, with love, with unspoken questions no one was ready to force.

Kramer waited, letting the silence breathe. Then he stepped closer, pulling a chair beside the bed. His voice was calm, careful, stripped of interrogation but firm with necessity.

"Asher," he said, leaning forward so his face filled the young man's blurred vision. "I need to ask you something. You don't have to tell me the whole story yet. But I need you to answer me plainly."

Asher's gaze found him to be heavy and deliberate.

Kramer's voice dropped. "Who assaulted you?"

The room went still. Robin clasped her hands tighter. Carolina's breath caught. Keith leaned forward, eyes locked on his son.

Asher's lips trembled. His chest rose once, shallow. Then the word came, slow but certain, like stone laid on stone:

"…Grayson… Rivers."

Carolina gasped, tears spilling fresh. Keith closed his eyes, his hand clutching the rail. Robin whispered, "Justice begins."

Kramer sat back, the faintest exhale escaping him. It wasn't a triumph. It wasn't even relief. It was confirmation of what he'd needed, what the case required, what the truth demanded.

The family leaned closer to Asher, whispering comfort, holding his hand, and smoothing his hair.

Kramer stood, giving them their moment. His jaw was set, his eyes sharp. The name was spoken now. The story would follow.

But in that hospital room, it was enough that the son who had been silent for so long had finally spoken.

Chapter 31: The Call

The holding cell was small but efficient: cinderblock painted the color of old paper, a steel bench bolted to the wall, and a narrow window with ballistic glass that let in a slice of afternoon light, much like a blade lets in light. The precinct's hum seeped through the door, phones, boots, the punctured laughter of men who had learned to joke in hallways to keep from rusting.

Grayson Rivers sat straight on the bench, suit jacket folded with careful exactness beside him, shirt cuffs turned back a clean inch. The fluorescent above him flickered once, decided against it, and steadied. He had slept sitting up in worse places: airports, boardrooms, a helicopter with a pilot who coughed between coordinates. This, too, was temporary. Most things were.

A clatter of keys, the metal groan of hinges. An officer opened the door and jerked his chin toward the hall. "Phone's free."

Rivers stood, lifted his jacket not to wear, but to keep it from the floor, and walked. The corridor smelled like aftershave and coffee that had boiled itself proud. On the wall by the phone, a laminated placard explained the rules in thick font: five minutes, recorded, subject to monitoring. A handset hung from a spiral cord that remembered every argument it had ever heard.

He picked it up. The line was cold. He dialed home.

It rang twice, then three times, then once more like the last step before a long drop: a click, a breath, her voice.

"Grayson?"

"Hello, love."

Marisol breathed out a sound that was half his name, half relief. "I didn't know if… The news…. There are vans outside, and they keep calling the house. I told the kids you had meetings." Her voice trembled, trying not to. "Is it true?"

He looked at the notice on the wall as if it were a painting he could critique. "I'm at the precinct. It's procedural."

"Procedural," she repeated, as if saying the word twice might make it choose a side. "They said 'arrested.' They said 'assault.' They said…" She stopped, as if giving the words more room would let them grow. "Tell me what to say to our children."

He rested his shoulder lightly against the cinderblock and closed his eyes just long enough to put the hall in order inside his head. "You'll tell Skylar I'm working late. He respects schedules; he'll respect that. You'll tell Brooklyn I'll read tomorrow night instead. She likes promises better than explanations. And you'll sing to the baby in the kitchen, because the tile makes your voice carry, and he settles when he hears the echo. Keep to the routine."

"Grayson," she whispered. "They're saying terrible things."

"They will say worse before they run out of breath," he said, and made the sentence gentle by choice. "Do not open the door to anyone. Do not answer unknown numbers. Let the house be a house."

Silence moved between them like a careful animal. He could hear the faintest sound behind her silverware being set down, a chair being pushed back, a child's voice in the distance asking if the cartoons were over. The life he had built for himself was there, close enough to file, far enough to be safe.

"Did you do it?" she asked. She kept her voice low, but the question rang like crystal. "Tell me you didn't. Tell me this is a mistake."

A red light above the phone glowed its small reminder: recorded, monitored. He could have said a hundred true things in that moment: what men had done for him; what he had never needed to touch with his own hands; how a city moves when you say now. He chose the thing that fit into the space allowed.

"This is a misunderstanding being made useful by my enemies," he said.

He heard the faint catch of breath that meant she was searching his words for a key and finding only locks. "Do you remember the first time they wrote about you?" she asked suddenly, surprising them both. "The paper called you disciplined. You cut it out, put it in a frame, hung it too low because you didn't measure first." A soft laugh, broken and lovely. "You said truth is the thing you can point to. I want to point to something."

He let the memory sit. The office floor had been raw concrete then, the windows unwashed, the furniture borrowed. He had believed more in momentum than in chairs. He had believed in her more than both. "Point to me," he said.

"I am," she answered. "That's why I'm asking."

The line went quiet, but it was not empty. He heard paper slide under a door somewhere down the hall, a stapler exhale. An officer's cough. He thought of how many men had asked for forgiveness through this handset, how many had promised reform as if time were theirs to rearrange.

"Listen carefully," he said, and the tone became a briefing without effort. "Tell Priya to freeze external communications, push the board meeting by forty-eight hours, and keep the compensation committee off the calendar until further notice. No statements from the company. None. If the press calls your phone, you smile into the silence and hang up. If anyone asks you what you know, you say you have confidence in due process and in me. Then you say nothing."

"I don't want to learn a script for this," she said, and the sadness in it felt heavier than anger could have. "I want my husband home."

"I will be," he said. "There's a process."

She let that word sit where it landed and looked at it from all sides. "Skylar asked if you're a bad guy," she said. "He learned that phrase from a movie he isn't supposed to watch. I told him we don't use those words in our house. I told him people are complicated. He asked if complicated men get to tuck their kids in."

A corner of his mouth lifted despite himself. "Tell him complicated men keep their promises." He kept his voice light. He kept it kind. "I'll read tomorrow night."

"If they let you."

"They will," he said, with the steadiness of a forecast.

A chime sounded down the hall, time shrinking. He had not yet asked about dinner, about which of the children had spilled sauce, or about whether the baby had discovered the bottom drawer again. He had not spoken the names; he called them when no one else was in the room. He had also not said the one sentence that would change her life more than any other. He tailored his silences with the same care he applied to a suit.

"Marisol," he said.

"I'm here," she answered, as if proximity could be expanded by intention.

"Look at the clock over the stove," he said. "Count out loud with the second hand if it helps. Then breathe. Make bedtime ordinary. Extraordinary nights break more than they need to."

"How can you sound like this?" she asked, not accusing, not admiring. "How can you be so calm?"

"Because I already did my fear," he said. "On another day, when it was useful."

She made a slight sound. It might have been a laugh. It might have been the opposite. "They say the man in charge never leaves fingerprints. Is that what you are now? A man without hands?"

The question was clean. He didn't flinch from clean things. "I am a man who keeps his family safe," he said.

"Then come home."

"I will," he repeated, and let the promise choose its own date.

Footsteps approached. A shadow lengthened across the floor and resolved into a figure with an upturned palm and the kind of patience that comes from repeating rules to men who survive by bending them.

"Thirty seconds," the officer said.

Rivers nodded once and shifted the handset just enough to change the sound of his breath. "The children?"

"Skylar is worried in straight lines," she said. "Brooklyn's worry loops. The baby forgets and remembers in ten-minute increments."

"Good," he said softly. "Let them each be themselves. Give Skylar a number to hold. Give Brooklyn a story. Give the baby your heartbeat."

A pause. He could see her in the kitchen in his mind, one hand on the counter, one hand around a glass she'd forgotten to drink from, the window over the sink offering a small rectangle of sky that could be any weather she needed it to be.

"I loved you before they wrote about you," she said, the words landing somewhere that didn't belong to law. "And after."

He let the sentence find him. He let it stand in the room like a person. He felt, not for the first time, the pull of a life that had no use for board minutes or hold music.

"Keep the door locked," he said. "Kiss them for me. I'll call again."

"Grayson," she whispered, urgent now, the edge of the world showing. "Just tell me…. are they right?"

He looked at the red light. He looked at the officer's hand. He looked at the small sign that said, 'All calls may be recorded.' Then he gave her the only answer that fit inside the frame he had chosen to live in.

"They have to prove it," he said.

The line clicked. Silence opened where her breath had been.

He stood there a moment longer with the dead receiver at his ear, listening to how nothing sounded when it had just been something. He set the handset back in its cradle with care, a quality he did not extend to his enemies, and stepped away from the wall.

"Time," the officer said, because the job asks you to tell the obvious often.

Rivers adjusted his cuffs out of habit and smoothed his shirt across his stomach. He did not ask for water. He did not ask to sit. He let the corridor fold him back into its rhythm and returned to the small room that made most men pace, but he did not.

He sat on the bench with his jacket folded, palms flat beside him so the chain lay quiet and uncomplaining. A narrow band of afternoon light cut across the window. He thought, *He's going to wish he were dead.* He leaned his head back against the concrete wall and cracked a faint, almost devious smile.

Epilogue: A Different Dawn

The days no longer blurred together. They stacked themselves like bricks, each one adding weight and shape to the structure of Asher's recovery. Morning light warmed the hospital blinds. The steady beep of the monitor had become less ominous, more like a metronome counting out his second chance.

He was no longer motionless. His hand could lift now, weak but deliberate, tracing the air toward the cup Carolina held for him. His eyes followed voices with a new sharpness, the fog lifting more each day. Words came slowly, haltingly, but they came.

Keith sat at his bedside every morning, his Bible unopened on his lap, too heavy with thoughts to read. When Asher whispered "Hi Dad" again, clearer this time, Keith's chest ached with a pride so tangled with regret that it left him breathless.

Robin was steady as always. She prayed aloud, then prayed quietly when she thought no one heard. Sometimes Asher turned his head toward her mid-prayer, eyes glassy but aware. She would stop, smile through tears, and tell him, "God isn't finished with you yet."

Carolina hovered closest, protective in her quiet way. She brushed his hair when it matted, dabbed his lips with water when his throat was too raw, and whispered things no one else could hear. He smiled for her, weak but real, as though remembering what it meant to be a brother before he had been anyone else.

Kramer stood in the doorway more often than he entered. He'd lean against the frame, arms crossed, taking in the sight of a man who had been as close to gone as anyone could be. He didn't intrude on the family's moments. But sometimes Asher's gaze found him, and Kramer would give the slightest nod, a detective's promise that the fight wasn't over.

One afternoon, when Keith stepped into the hall to call Marisol with an update, Kramer entered quietly. He pulled the chair closer and sat down.

"Asher," he said, his voice steady. "You don't have to give me everything right now. But when you're ready, your words will matter."

Asher's lips parted. The effort was visible, his brow furrowed with the strain of lifting syllables into the air. "He…did it."

Kramer leaned in, not to press, but to reassure. "I know. You said his name. That was enough for now."

A flicker of relief crossed Asher's face. He closed his eyes briefly, then opened them again, his hand twitching faintly toward Kramer's. The detective let the gesture stand without touching it, a gesture of respect in a room already thick with love.

News moved differently outside the hospital walls. Headlines turned bold, radio stations repeated the same clip of Grayson Rivers walking out of his tower in cuffs. His employees defended him in interviews, calling him "a visionary" and "a good man." Commentators debated whether the charges would stick, whether this was justice or ambition in uniform.

In the quiet corners, though, the truth took root. Subpoenas spread like cracks in ice. Financial records surfaced, cold and damning. Croft's name appeared on paper where Rivers had kept his own hands clean. Charles and Ray, each in their own cells, began to weigh years against sentences.

And Rivers himself, still in a tailored calm even behind bars, made his one call to his wife and ended it with words that rattled in the ears of anyone listening: "They have to prove it."

He had chosen denial. Asher had chosen truth. The trial ahead would decide which had more weight in the world men built.

Weeks later, Asher took his first steps with the help of a physical therapist, his family watching from the hall. His body trembled, his jaw clenched, sweat beading across his forehead, but he moved. Two steps. Then three. Then, four steps before he collapsed back into the chair.

The room erupted in cheers, tears, and laughter. Robin whispered, "Hallelujah." Carolina clapped, her joy uncontained. Keith bowed his head and let the tears come openly, no longer ashamed.

Asher looked up, exhausted, but with a smile. "I'm…still here," he whispered.

"Yes, you are," Carolina said fiercely. "And you're not alone."

That evening, Kramar stood outside the hospital, the city lights blinking alive as dusk settled. He cradled a Styrofoam cup of cold coffee, holding it more for the ritual than the taste. Old habits had ways of finding you when the work piled high.

He thought of the pond, of a man dragged broken into water, of silence almost winning. He thought of Rivers sitting calmly in his cell, untouched by fear, waiting for proof. He thought of the family upstairs, tired, fractured, but bound together by something heavier than pride.

For the first time in months, he allowed himself a small, weary smile.

The case was far from finished. The trial loomed. Testimony would be hard, painful, and dangerous. But the witness was alive. The family was together. The river, however dark, had not swallowed him.

Kramer dropped the cup into the trash bin, shoved his hands into his pockets, and started back inside.

In the hospital room, Asher slept, his breathing even, his family gathered close. The blinds shifted in the evening breeze, casting thin bars of shadow across his face. Carolina traced a line along his wrist, Robin whispered another prayer, and Keith sat steady by the rail.

And somewhere in the silence, unspoken but certain, was the truth:

A man who once believed he was the exception had faced the cost of his pride.

A family that feared they had lost him now had him back.

And the city, scarred but unbroken, waited for the day when the name Grayson Rivers would no longer carry power, only judgment.

The End.

Author's Note

When I first began writing The Table of Regrets: What Was Too Much?, I didn't realize how closely Asher's story would reflect the struggle many of us face in our own time. His journey is fictional, but the sins that weighed him down are all too real.

This book was never just about crime, power, or even family. At its heart, it is about what happens when human desire grows unchecked, when wanting more becomes a way of life. The Bible calls this gluttony, though in our culture, we've often reduced the word to eating too much food. But gluttony is so much broader than that. It is the sin of excess. It is the belief that if one is good, ten must be better. It is the hunger that never says enough.

Asher's downfall was gluttony disguised as success. His appetite was for recognition, power, and control. He convinced himself he was untouchable, the exception to every rule. Pride fed that gluttony, and together they hollowed him out. He thought he was building an empire, but in truth, he was building a table of regrets, one bad choice laid upon another, until the weight nearly crushed him.

We see this same pattern in our world today. Social media tells us we are only as valuable as the likes we collect. Advertisements whisper that happiness is just one more purchase away. Our culture often glorifies hustle, status, and wealth at the expense of peace, relationships, and integrity.

The result? We gorge ourselves on things that cannot satisfy, and we starve our souls of the truth that could set us free.

The Bible warns in Philippians 3:19 KJV of those "whose end is destruction, whose God is their belly, and whose glory is in their shame, who mind earthly things." That verse is not only about food, but also about living for appetites that can never be filled. Asher's story echoes this truth. He believed success would satisfy him, but success only demanded more. He thought money would save him, but money only deepened his debts. He felt that power would protect him, but it ultimately betrayed him.

But God's Word does not leave us in despair. Romans 13:13-14 KJV urges us to "walk honestly, as in the day, not in rioting and drunkenness, not in chambering and wantonness, not in strife and envying. But put ye on the Lord Jesus Christ, and make not provision for the flesh, to fulfil the lusts thereof."

Asher's turning point came not when his body broke, but when he realized he was not the exception. That moment, when he sat at the table of his regrets and chose truth over pride, is the exact moment available to us today. We may not sit in a hospital bed or a police interrogation room, but each of us faces choices. Each of us must decide: Will I keep feeding the appetites of this world, or will I choose life, choose truth, choose Christ?

I wrote this story not only as a thriller, but as a mirror. It is meant to entertain, yes, but also to challenge. If you saw yourself in Asher's hunger for more, in his inability to say enough, then know this: you are not alone. And you are not without hope.

Joshua 24:15 KJV reminds us, "Choose you this day whom ye will serve…but as for me and my house, we will serve the Lord." That was Asher's final choice in this story. It can also be yours.

May the Table of Regrets warn of excess and point us to the God who sets a better table, one filled with hope, never regrets. May you never face the question: What Was Too Much?

Acknowledgments

I want to thank God first and foremost for His grace and guidance throughout every word of this book.

To my family thank you for your patience, prayers, and unwavering love. You are my greatest inspiration and the foundation of my work.

Scripture Credits

All Scripture quotations are taken from the King James Version (KJV) of the Bible.

About the Author

Kimberly Cummings is the author of the Red Cover Collection of Christian suspense and drama, including I'm Not Him: The Stranger in the Mirror Was Me, The Waiting Porch: Finding Your Way Back, Love Only Me, Through the Storms: A Journey of Faith, Hope, and Perseverance, and A Different Echo: Tiny Words. Her novels weave suspense, family struggles, and spiritual truths into stories that challenge readers to reflect deeply on faith, redemption, and the consequences of their choices.

Beyond writing, Kimberly is passionate about encouraging others through faith-based storytelling, speaking engagements, and community outreach. Her mission is to bring hope, healing, and courage to those facing life's storms while pointing them back to the God of second chances.

She lives in Ohio, where she balances her roles as an author, entrepreneur, and mentor. When she's not writing, she enjoys teaching, building her publishing brand, The Cozy Scratchpad, and spending time with her family.

Connect with Kimberly online:

🌐 www.kimberlycummingsauthor.com

📷 Instagram: @Scratchpadcreate

📚 Amazon Author Page:
https://business.amazon.com/abredir/author/thecozyscratchpad